ALL THE PETTY MYTHS

Curated by M.H. Norris

ALL THE PETTY MYTHS
An 18thWall Productions book published by
arrangement with M.H. Norris
verba mea in minibus
desiderium meum
Cover by Pamela Best and Shoshana Radka
Frontspiece by Pamela Best
Design by SJS Design

To The Doctor Who Nerds,
James and Nikki—
Thank you for helping me turn this
idea into reality.

Table of Contents

Introduction

M.H. Norris

Dr. Rosella Tassoni will not tell you whether or not the ghost is real.

Go ahead, ask her, make her day. Chances are, she'll give you a look and tell you it's not her job.

The stories inside of this book tell tales of how crime was mixed with mythology and the preternatural. Yes, I said preternatural and not supernatural. Trust me, you don't want to mix those terms up in Rosella's presence.

All the Petty Myths has been something that's been in the works since around the time that 18thWall Productions put out its first book. From initial concept to the finished product you now hold in your hands, this has been such a fun process.

I introduce you to Dr. Rosella Tassoni in *Midnight*. That story very quickly became bigger than I thought it was and this story is a backdoor pilot into her very own series named after the title of this book.

What does Rosella do?

Well, that I'm going to leave for her to tell you. If I ruin her fun she might get cranky with me and there's nothing worse than trying to write a book with a cranky muse.

Marc Sorondo has contributed to a few 18thWall anthologies and I'm glad that I get to include him in *All the Petty Myths*. His tale, "Locked Room," includes what the title indicates, a Locked Room Mystery featuring what appears to be a ghost.

Is the ghost real?

Rosella would like to remind you again that that's not her job.

James Bojaciuk's story, "Dopplegangers (And Other Artistic Piffle)," was a special request from me. After having the opportunity to be a part of 18thWall Productions' *Science of Deduction* series, I asked our resident Holmes expert to write me a tale from that era.

An anthology about mysteries and the preternatural would not be complete without a tale involving a vanishing hitchhikers and D. J. Tyrer's story "Tutle and Gretle" brings us just that. He took an interesting take on the tale and I found it to be a fun read.

Are the ghosts within the pages of this anthology real?

For the last time, Rosella would like to remind you that that is *not* in her job description.

Midnight

M.H. Norris

Dr. Rosella Tassoni looked over the auditorium full of half-asleep freshmen and quickly remembered why she *usually* only agreed to lecture upper-level courses.

"Since the beginning of time, man has told stories. When a written language came along, these were written down. Some would surpass their own cultures, becoming what we know to be legends. Today we call the study of those legends mythology. Every culture has their own distinct legends, yet many share a similar foundation. Max Müller considered these legends 'a disease of language,' but clearly they're something more. I prefer Tolkien's explanation for legends in his essay 'On Fairy-Stories,' originally delivered to students very similar to you. 'The history of fairy-stories is probably more complex than the physical history of the human race, and as complex as the history of human language.'"

Rosella clicked the slide over. "What are the origins of, as Tolkien would call them, 'fairy-stories'? 'I am too unlearned to deal with this question in any other way than with a few remarks…It is plain enough that fairy- stories (in wider or in narrower sense) are very ancient indeed. Related things appear in very early records; and they are found universally, wherever there is language. We are therefore obviously confronted with a variant of the problem that the archaeologist encounters, or the comparative philologist: with the debate between independent evolution (or rather invention) of the similar; inheritance from a common ancestry; and diffusion at various times from one or more centres."

Turning away from the screen she studied the crowd. "Tolkien is considered one of the greatest fantasy writers in the history of mankind. His books are still widely read and have inspired Academy-Award-winning movies and a popular MMORPG."

That comment helped her pick out the gamers in the audience by their grins. She could tell a couple of them were thinking about playing that as soon as class was over. In fact, the way one boy's head shot up, she couldn't help but wonder if she looked at his screen if she would find Middle-Earth.

"But, more than that, he was one of the great philologists, with an intense knowledge of language's history—and the mythology that has always clung to it. *Gilgamesh*, after all, is our earliest surviving written record. Tolkien acknowledged Müller's quote though and had this to say, 'Max Müller's view of mythology as a 'disease of language' can be abandoned without regret. Mythology is not a disease at all, though it may, like all human things, become diseased. You might as well say that thinking is a disease of the mind. It would be more near the truth to say that languages, especially modern

European languages, are a disease of mythology.'"

That caused her to chuckle. "I prefer to agree with Tolkien on this. After all, that quote is how I earn my living, in a sense."

As she walked across the stage, clicking through slides, she eyed one of the students. He slipped into the back of the lecture hall, border-lining the time that it was socially acceptable to arrive late. Which was, also, the time it was polite for Rosella to be late. She'd earned her doctorate. At least according to the old myth— Rosella preferred to be on time to speaking events, not in the mood to waste not only her time but the time of those listening. The student quickly opened his laptop and tried to look attentive. His face appeared to be relaxed, but his clenched jaw told her he was stressed and a little over focused on the task at hand. Not only that—but she could see his wire from here. He must be new, he was too tense. That or he hadn't been warned that she was pretty good at reading body language. But seriously, Quantico was slipping if they thought that act was covert. She assumed he was wired simply to test him in the field, in a safe situation. *Baby's first op.*

"Some stories are to teach a lesson, it's the reason we have fables and how Aesop became a household name. Others are fun stories to tell around a campfire.

"Others take a darker side. Or, rather, people choose to let them." Another click, another slide.

"Serial killers have been popularized, lately, with the influx of 'realistic' crime dramas.

Because of this same dramas, people are obsessed with the idea of the forensic sciences."

Now she had their attention.

"Sometimes, the two meet. Killers think they can hide behind the myths. Forensic Mythology if you will."

A student in the fourth row raised her hand and Rosella nodded to her. Being called on by a guest would at least give her a good story. She was one of the ones who'd perked up at the mention of *Lord of the Rings Online*. Her Mac was plastered with stickers—a TARDIS design that went out with the sixties, a *Metropolitan* press badge reading Smith, and Mara Jade holding a pink lightsaber aloft. Her straight posture and over-eager expression let Rosella know that this was probably one of her friend's better students. *Definitely* the sort to get a thrill out of a guest's attention.

"So, you're saying that most urban myths aren't true?"

Rosella smiled. "That's not my job to figure out; that was more something Margaret McConnell studied to learn, and I direct you to her books. I prefer to leave that to other people to argue over. I have to sort the very real killer from the myth."

Another hand, this time from a boy who had looked bored until she had said "serial killers." Then his attitude changed rather quickly and the combination of that, along with the book by Temperance Brennan in his bag, made her wonder if he knew how much was real and how much was fiction. Though at least he was reading one of the *more* accurate adaptations. Nodding to him, she was partially curious what question he'd come up with.

"How do the two manage to come together? Mythology's just stories. Forensic Science is an actual science."

It was a question she often got. With a nod she clicked a slide. "Most people wonder how I manage to see the two combined. Who here has gotten one of those annoying chain emails, the ones that say if you don't pass it on you'll bad luck or meet an untimely demise?"

Hands all over the auditorium went up.

"A few years ago in Dallas, Texas, one of those went around. The thing was, people who didn't pass it along met said untimely demise."

She clicked a slide and showed a set of three victims. Each one had received a single a single .22 shot to the head. A tarot baring the reverse chariot was laid beside them.

"All of our victims had received that email within twenty-four hours of their death. For a while that was our only tie between victims. Forensic Science—the wound delivered at point blank, the presence of the card. Forensic Mythology—the email, and the card itself. When reversed, the chariot tarot card means bad luck."

"Did you catch the guy?" Someone near the back asked without raising their hand.

"Eventually. He managed to kill five victims before we were able to nail down his location. But when killers use something like these superstitious emails or urban legends, they often

15

use them as a mask to hide their crimes. Some people are so focused on the legend coming true that they refuse to see what's right in front of them—a human being."

"So the myths aren't true?" The over-eager girl repeated her earlier question.

"Once again, I didn't say that. It's not my business to prove or disprove them. Though I will say those annoying emails are probably the creation of someone who had too much time on their hands and more than enough access to the internet."

That earned her a few chuckles.

"Forensic Mythology is an emerging sub-classification of the forensic sciences. And while many of my colleagues don't think it's practical, I do know that it has helped to save lives and bring peace to victims."

Another hand went up and she nodded to the person about halfway back. "But why mythology? What made you think to combine it with the forensic sciences?"

Rosella launched into her traditional lecture, smiling at how once again, she had managed to get the students to steer the conversation to where she wanted to go. Of course, they didn't realize that that's what just happened.

The rest of the class passed quickly and soon enough students were packing up to rush off to their next class, a hot date, a procrastinated study session, or one of the seemingly endless things students could do. Finally, the tardy student from earlier made his way up, carrying a copy of her latest book in his hand.

"You know, you can drop the cover now. A tip, when your body language sends mixed signals, a trained eye is going to notice."

The kid's face dropped and he shrugged. "Does that mean you won't sign my book?"

Rosella let out a chuckle. "I'll sign it. I'm assuming somewhere in that bag there's a file for me?"

"A case came up and my professor wanted you to take a look…"

"Your professor knows that, officially, I'm not here." Rosella let out a sigh, the extremely long to-do list she had made for this trip to DC suddenly seeming unattainable.

"According to him, it's right up your alley. He'll touch base, see if he can get you a consulting gig."

She turned to Professor Alicia Walter, an old friend of hers. "I might have to take a raincheck on that coffee."

A large can of salt—the brand gave away that it had been bought at the local dollar store—sat beside a pillar candle in a glass drawer. It was probably of the same origin of its twin, which lay tipped over beside a taped silhouette. It gave Rosella a hint of the sad story that had played out here.

Rosella rubbed over a bloodstain with a gloved hand and didn't try to hold in a sigh.

"I don't get it." She turned to see the Sheriff Kristopher Peake studying her studying the scene. "I've seen it so many times and I still don't get it."

She pulled the case file out of her bag and looked at the picture of fifteen-year-old Ashley Coats. Honor Roll, freshman at Huntington Prep, involved with the SGA. A fairly large amount of friends on Facebook, a couple hundred followers on Twitter. All the shallow signs of stability. Nothing indicated that something like this could happen to her.

But that silhouette proved otherwise.

Five kids, five crime scenes, all within just a few hours of each other on a Friday night. The salt and the candle gave away that it was a ritual of some kind.

What had Ashley gotten into?

She opened the file again as she heard someone enter the room.

"Who is she?" a voice asked the Sheriff.

"Someone the FBI called in. Apparently, she's an expert on cases like this."

"And we weren't consulted?"

"We have jurisdiction here."

Rosella looked at the photos of the crime scene and noticed that Ashley was cut open, hence the large blood stain on the floor. "And we have a group of dead kids and no evidence that this *isn't* going to happen again so if you are going to act like small children can you at least do it outside and let me work? Thank you."

She wandered into the kitchen, mentally ticking off different cultures, different rituals, but it was always a mix of what was and what wasn't there. She opened the cabinets until she found the spices. Garlic, oregano, cilantro—nothing outside the usual household collection.

Shutting the cabinets, she walked around the kitchen peeking in the pantry.

"All the internal organs were missing when the coroner came, right?" She walked past the group of law enforcement officers to the other side of the house. "From all of the victims?"

"Wasn't a pretty sight."

Rosella nodded as she continued to wander the house. Matches littered the floor in a couple of places. Looking at the notes, she searched for the time of death. The coroner estimated it to be around three in the morning. She added discussing a few things with him to her mental to-do list.

That time of death *did* narrow down the ritual some more.

She wandered into the bathroom, peeking in the drawers and cabinets. But nothing in Ashley's bathroom showed anything outside of the ordinary for a girl her age.

The parents' room was first, but looked basically untouched. "Where are her parents?"

"Staying with some friends until after the funeral on Wednesday," an officer, who had been bagging something in Ashley's room, answered.

"Have they been here since?"

"Briefly."

Rosella peeked inside the mother's closet, the faint hint of designer perfume lingering on her clothes. The closet was all women's clothes; the husband's must have been in a guest room. There was another match off to the side of the master bathroom floor.

She made her way into the girl's room, not surprised at the hottie-of-the-month's face all over her walls. CDs took a shelf where books should be, and her laptop sat on her bed. With a groan, she saw every season of *Supernatural. Of course* she watched that show. Victims in Rosella's line always seemed to. Next to it sat a couple of seasons of *American Duos* and Rosella quickly shoved away the nagging feeling that she'd forgotten to TiVo it.

Right now, she needed to focus.

As she crossed the threshold, she looked down and saw a piece of paper. In flowing script was Ashley's name and a drop of blood.

That *really* narrowed it down.

Rosella knocked on the door three times. Wood.

There were a couple more matches by the door.

"Make sure you bag up the matches we're finding all over the floor."

Coming into the room, she looked under the bed, between the mattress and the pad, between books, and in the drawers. Besides the things at the door, this room could have belonged to any teenager.

"What's the verdict?"

Rosella turned to see the Sheriff leaning up against the doorframe of the parent's room.

"Sometimes, when figuring out what ritual, it's a mix of what's there or what's not there."

"A ritual?" The Sheriff looked troubled. "What do you mean?"

"The salt, the candles, it was a ritual. There were several options that would require both of those. Actually, most preternatural related, modern rituals require both."

"Preternatural, don't you mean *supernatural*?"

Rosella crossed her arms as she felt her eyebrow reach for her hairline. "Would people stop misusing that term? This was a *preternatural* ritual."

Seeing the blank look on his face—she sighed, and slipped into lecture mode. "Preternatural is used to refer to actions that are demonic in nature. Supernatural refers to acts of God. The word is often bastardized into meaning 'things beyond nature.'"

"You're saying she was practicing witchcraft?"

"I am not."

"Summing this up, demons had something to do with this? But she didn't practice witchcraft."

Staring the man down, she decided to cut him a break, for now. "Ashley here unknowingly engaged into a preternatural ritual. In fact, I'm fairly certain I know which one it is."

"What is it?"

Rosella made her way back into the family room where the silhouette still sat on the floor. "It looks like she summoned the Midnight Man. And he won the game."

Rosella stepped outside Ashley's house as her phone rang. "Tassoni."

She listened to the caller on the other hand, the landlord for one of the offices she'd been looking at. With a sigh, she rescheduled the appointment, hoping some of her favorite spaces weren't leased before she could make it back to Washington.

"I'll let you know when I get back to town." Rosella told the woman on the other end. The woman started mentioning a few other properties that were coming empty. Pulling out her evidence pad, she jotted down some of the details.

A car pulled up and she saw a pair of people exit, eyeing her. Great, her FBI leash had shown up. She'd hoped she would have a little more time before they figured out which crime scene she went to.

"Ummhmmm." She jotted down more information about the properties as the pair, a man and a woman, walked up to her. It was easy for her to tell which one she would get along with and which one she wouldn't. The woman was trying to joke around with the man as they came up the walk. The man on the other hand was eyeing her phone, his face wondering how she dared to take a call at a crime scene.

"I'll let you know when I will get back to Washington. Thanks for being so understanding." She hung up and turned, placing a fake smile on her face. "Sorry about that. Dr. Rosella Tassoni."

She held out her hand and the woman shook it. "Special Agent Aubrey Wednesday. This is my partner, Special Agent Alexander Pugsley."

Oh the jokes she could make with those last names. Something told her it wasn't the best idea.

"Pleasure." She held out her hand to Agent Pugsley who stared, then finally shook it. This was going to be fun. "I've walked this crime scene already but if you care to join me, I'll share some of my observations with you. I'm sure your superiors are anxious to create a preliminary profile."

Leading them back inside, she pointed out some of the signs of the ritual before pulling out her file and pointing out some of the preliminary findings from the coroner. "I'm planning to visit the morgue next to take a look at the bodies to confirm some of my suspicions. That and make sure we're only dealing with one myth here."

"One?" Agent Wednesday looked at her.

"Some UnSubs mix and match legends. Sometimes it's to build their own legend. You wouldn't believe how many killers I've met who see this as some game to stoke their own ego. At any rate, the organs. I'm curious why the UnSub took them." Rosella looked once more at the preliminary report. "Anything else you two need here?"

Biting down a sigh, Rosella signed in with the receptionist. A man who looked to be old enough to be her father stepped out. "Dr. Tassoni?"

She nodded and he made his way over, shaking her hand. "Dr. Felix Crowdell."

"Do you have any additional information that you didn't provide in your preliminary report?" Rosella fell in step beside him.

"Toxicology came back from the lab this morning. Turns out all five victims had the same hallucinogenic drug in their system. Flekka. Only really in Florida right now. Easy to make, and known for its horror movie, grindhouse hallucinations. Every trip a bad trip, guaranteed." He handed her a piece of paper and she skimmed the results. Another clue that led to the Midnight Game. "I'm waiting for some test results to come back. The way he left these victims has limited my results, I'm afraid."

Rosella nodded. "I'm curious to see how he left them when he took the organs. It could eliminate a few possibilities."

"They say you're a mythology expert?"

Rosella smiled at yet another tentative inquiry into her work. "I'm a Forensic Mythologist."

"Is that actually a thing?"

"It will be."

Dr. Crowdell paused at the door. "In here. I've kept them together to assist you all in your investigation."

He opened it and with the other hand waved her in and she grabbed a pair of gloves out of the container by the door. Five stretchers took up most of the room's space but Rosella could still move around comfortably. "Are they in any order?"

"As best as I can determine, they are in chronological order."

Lifting off the sheet off the body on the far side of the room, Rosella took a second to look at the tag attached to the toe. Edwin Finnegan, a year older than Ashley, from the same school. So far, that was the best link the FBI had. Pulling the sheet back to his waist, Rosella examined the gaping wound that left most of the abdomen open.

"Your report said you believed this was done with a knife."

"Near as I can tell."

One person has a fair amount of organs. Five people have a ton. What could he need with five sets of organs? Another ritual? A few possibilities came to mind. She clicked her tongue, making a mental calculation there was no full moon on Halloween this year. More ordinarily, the black market wouldn't be upset if these wandered their way. Replacing the cloth, she made her way to another victim, Shay Hanley. The gaping wound was different.

"The UnSub took the reproductive organs from the female victims. Another thing to note is that all the organs were taken rather haphazardly. They didn't know what they were doing. Does that mean something?"

Rosella studied the wound, running a finger along its edge, trying to get a feel for the knife. "I can't be sure right now, besides it knocking out anyone with extensive knowledge of anatomy and physiology. All five between midnight and four?"

"As best I can tell. Sam Watts wasn't even found until Monday morning."

"They were found sporadically all weekend," Rosella said more to herself than to Dr. Crowdell.

"Is that significant?"

"Anything could be significant." Rosella studied a series of bruises on Sam. "What about these bruises? Antemortem or Postmortem?"

"Antemortem. Some might be from a fight, but to be honest, I can't know for sure."

She studied them another moment. "They could be from running into things, if my theory is right."

She walked into the station's homicide bullpen to find it in a state of organized chaos. On the far side of the room she saw Agents Pugsley and Wednesday working in a conference room with a handful of people. Before she could make it to them, she was stopped by Sheriff Peake. "We've got you set up in Conference Room B."

He led her to a room next to the FBI's and she nodded at the setup. A white board and a bulletin board sat on the far side of a table that could seat at least six. "I'm going to need to interview the families. Let the school know I'll be stopping by either today or tomorrow. It's already Wednesday and we don't know for sure that this UnSub won't strike again, come Friday."

The Sheriff nodded, leaving her alone in the conference room. A minute later, an officer came in and left her a box of information. She shut the door, pulled out her laptop and set it up to the station's Wi-Fi before putting on some classical music.

Two boards awaited her. She quickly pulled up the research she already had on the Midnight Game, found out the code to the printer, and printed it off. Next came the victims…

Five kids, different ages, different genders, different ethnicities, same school. Maybe she should visit the school sooner rather than later. Three girls, two boys, ages fifteen through eighteen. Crime scene photos confirmed that all five had been playing the Midnight Game, but Rosella made a mental note to go walk the remaining houses today.

"Dr. Tassoni?" A woman who looked as if she was straight out of the academy stuck her head in the door. "I'm Officer Gina Farnworth. They asked me to make sure you had everything you needed, and to let you know I'm available if you need me."

"Thanks, Gina. Can you get me copies of the local paper going back the last two weeks. And the school paper as well?"

"Of course." Officer Farnworth nodded before leaving the conference room.

Rosella took a step back from her victim board seeing if the pictures would somehow give her some insight into this crime. Why were these five playing the same game in five different locations on the same night? Were others playing? If so, why?

And if others were playing, why were these five killed?

Right now, she knew she had more questions than answers and made her way into the FBI's conference room. "Do we have anything from the kids' browser history?"

"Our tech guys are going over it now. We should have the results soon."

Rosella nodded and headed out. For now, she knew there was no point to sitting around here. She walked back outside to the rental car.

"Dr. Tassoni, is it true that the FBI are stuck on the case and resorted to calling you in?" One of the reporters called out and Rosella had to bite back the urge to snap as she forced herself into 'reporter mode.'

"The FBI are following several leads and requested my help with one."

"Is there a chance that the Friday Fiend will strike again?" Another reporter.

"We are unsure if the UnSub will strike again. Students should exercise caution until they are caught. No more questions." Rosella made her way to her car and hopped in, hoping to follow a few leads before the national press figured out she was here.

"Thanks for letting me into your school. I wanted to come after the students left to get a feel for the building. Then I'm going to come back tomorrow when school is in session and do another sweep. So far, this is the biggest tie we have to the five victims."

Both made their way over to the memorial. The victims faced her yet again. Ashley campaigning. Sam playing football. Brooke at

Prom last year with friends. Edwin in the marching band. Shay in the school play. None were traditional targets, and all were missed.

So far, she was just managing to have more questions than answers. "If you wouldn't mind giving me a tour and then getting me a copy of the victims' schedules, I would greatly appreciate it."

For the next hour she let the principal lead her around his school, pointing out lockers, homerooms, cafeteria, gym, auditorium, band room, and outdoor facilities. Flyers announcing the first dance of the school year littered the halls.

Nothing about this place seemed to scream out Midnight Game, and none of the five seemed like the type. Of course, Rosella knew that wasn't an indicator. Getting schedules, she made her way outside and back to the memorial just as her phone rang.

Biting back a groan, she answered the phone. She'd been avoiding this all day. "Hey, mom."

"I forgot, what time does your flight land tomorrow night?"

"About that." Rosella walked around the memorial, studying it in case it hid something. "I'm not going to make it home this weekend."

"But we need you back here. Your father and I have the Frisco wedding this weekend and we need all hands on deck. Plus Lapo and Celinia were so looking forward to seeing you. You know their son Edoardo is single—"

With a sigh, Rosella hit the FaceTime button and in a minute her mom's face appeared.

Pushing the button so that her mom could see the memorial, she said, "Mom, I can't leave."

"Five of them?" Her mom's voice was hushed and Rosella switched the camera back around.

"I know you and dad think I'm going to take over the bakery someday, but I can give these kids their voices back…and so many others after them. I'm good at this."

"But we need you here."

"But they need me here. I've got to go, mom."

Rosella hung up, and noticed a girl standing there, eyes red from tears shed as she clutched a framed photo.

"Can you catch who did this?" She handed the photo to Rosella who saw it was of the girl and Shay. "We went into Manhattan over the summer and saw a show and did some shopping. She was so excited because they were going to do *Beauty and the Beast* for the spring musical this year and wished it would come back on Broadway. So she could see it for inspiration."

"I'm going to do my best to catch them. Dr. Rosella Tassoni." She held out her hand.

"Hillary Langdon." The girl shook her hand before setting the photo in the memorial. "Shay and I have been best friends since Kindergarten."

"I'm sorry for your loss." Rosella watched the grieving girl. "When was the last time you talked to Shay?"

"A few hours before this happened. Maybe around eleven? She said something about

30

playing some game she'd heard about on The Nest. I was watching a movie so we hung up pretty quickly."

"The Nest?"

Hillary pulled out her phone and showed Rosella a Facebook-like site. "Some kids in the senior web-design class made it last year. The class kept it up this year."

Rosella studied the site before reaching in her bag and handing Hillary a business card. "Thanks for showing me this."

Rosella rushed back into the station and stopped at the FBI's conference room. "Have you ever heard of The Nest?"

"The what?"

"Tell your tech guys to hurry up. I ran into Shay Hanley's best friend when I stopped by the school. She said that Shay said that she was going to play a game she'd found on there."

Even Agent Pugsley showed some surprise, and she hadn't managed to get much more than indifference from him so far. "What's the Nest?"

"The school has its own Facebook. I'm sure all of our victims have an account on there." With that, Rosella made her way to the conference room. Sitting on the table were two stacks of newspapers. Nothing like some bedtime reading to get to sleep at night.

Grabbing the top paper off of one of the stacks, she sat down and flipped through it. The school paper was usually pretty short, and with only two issues a week, it was the easiest to go through. Sam Watt's name came up pretty quickly. Apparently he had some college scouts looking at him. He might have gone places.

Nothing really stood out to Rosella but, grudgingly, she had to admit—until she had a clearer picture, she might be looking a clue in the face and not know it. The local paper didn't hold much either, but it did let her see how they'd been covering the murders. More shock than substance, as usual.

She walked over to her board and wrote down some observations.

The Nest might provide clues.

She wanted to visit some classes and some teachers tomorrow. But there was the looming question—would this UnSub strike again on Friday night? It was already Wednesday, but she couldn't help that she'd just been called in.

And there was the Midnight Game. It was one she'd noted since it liked to show up on creepypasta and other myth sites, off and on. Personally, she didn't see the appeal in a game that made you wander around in the dark for almost four hours.

The UnSub must have looked at a variety of source material because it wasn't clear as to what happened if you were caught, but he had seemed to cover a bunch of eventualities. There was a hallucinogenic drug in all of the victim's systems. And it wasn't a local mix. The ME said something about it being a blend popular in Florida. Whoever this was went through a lot of trouble.

The bodies were also missing their internal organs. Why? What was the UnSub doing with all of them? Black market?

New cases brought more questions than answers. She would have to keep an eye out. Going out into the bullpen, she saw Officer Farnworth typing away on her computer. "Gina?"

She quickly turned. "Is there something I can help you with?"

"Keep an ear out for any chatter about someone being removed from the organ donation list without dying or receiving a transplant."

"Will do."

This early, Rosella had no idea if she was chasing a red herring or making progress. It was like working a thousand piece puzzle. You did it bit by bit and worked your way to the end.

Eyeing the five pictures hanging on the board, Rosella bit her lip.

Standing back up, Rosella went back into the FBI's conference room. "What do you know about The Midnight Game?"

"The what?" Agent Pugsley looked up from his pile of paper, looking as if he'd swallowed a sour lemon.

"It's honestly nothing more than a game created by someone with too much time on their hands and too much access to the internet. They then proceed to dress it up as an 'ancient pagan ritual.'" Rosella smiled as she slipped into lecture mode.

"The problem with this comes when you attempt to dig into it. It came to my attention about five years ago. So for the sake of curiosity, I did a little digging. No such pagan ritual exists. Nor does this game exist before it appeared on the pages of Creepypasta sites."

Agent Wednesday looked up from the notepad she'd been taking notes on. "What's this Midnight Game?"

"It's a two-fold thing. Before the clock strikes twelve, you must write out your full name and let a drop of your own blood rest on it, soaking into the paper. Then make sure all the lights are off in the house before sitting in front of a closed wooden door. Light your candle, knock on the door twenty-two times. The last time must be on the stroke of Midnight. Then open the door, blow out the candle, and then close the door again. Yes, that's nearly impossible to do in the space of time provided. No, that doesn't seem to have occurred to its creator.

"That's when the game begins. You must immediately relight your candle. After all, you've invited the Midnight Man into your house."

Agent Pugsley interrupted. "Who's the Midnight Man?"

"Depends on what you want to believe. I've seen some people pick apart the idea. Going back to the 'pagan' roots of the game one might argue that you've just summoned an angry god whose purpose is to discipline you for some supposed wrong. The text only defines him as an 'avenger.'"

Agent Wednesday nodded. "So you summon him at the stroke of midnight and then what?"

Rosella couldn't hold back a sarcastic laugh. "Then comes the reason that I think this is one of the most ridiculous things to hit the internet in a long time. You proceed to wander all around the dark house until 3:33 AM."

"That's oddly specific."

Rosella shrugged. "Another thing that leads credence to the fact that this is nothing more than something created by people looking to spook others with a goofy game. While there are records of people using a primitive form of a sundial in Egypt around 1500 BC it would be almost two millennia before mankind began telling time in a way that would be exact enough to consider playing this kind of game. The Romans had more precise time-telling, but that would hardly help."

"What happens if you get caught?" Agent Pugsley asked, looking at their evidence board.

"You're looking at the most popular theories. No one place has the answer to that. Some say he just causes you to hallucinate your worst nightmares. Others say he takes your organs."

"Why?"

Rosella shrugged. "Who knows? Does some mythical being need a reason?"

"You can't believe in this?" Agent Pugsley gave her a look.

"It's not my job to prove if the myths are real or not. My job is to help you forensically link the crime to the myth."

She turned to leave but paused in the doorway. "But why they picked this myth is beyond me."

Sipping on a tea that probably had more sugar in it than most people would think sane, Rosella made her way up the stairs of Huntington Prep. Her watch let her know that classes wouldn't start for another twenty minutes which gave her enough time to get a feel for the place.

In her years of freelance forensic anthropology, Rosella had been in and out of dozen of high schools, and in her opinion: you saw one you saw them all. That, or they just started to blur together. Just inside the front door were signs announcing the next football game, requests to join the drama club, the debate club, various smaller and fringe clubs, particularly ones for small sci-fi fandoms. She chuckled at seeing a *Doctor Who* club. Homecoming was already looking for volunteers.

Nothing indicated that this school would face tragedy, let alone the one it had faced less than a week ago. But the memorial outside, and the pictures of the victims, told another tale that was drastically different from the traditional trimmings of high school.

Taking a sip of her tea, she fought back a yawn.

Why did school start so early?

Already, the hallways were filling up with students who were getting ready to start another day. The odd looks she got let her know that these students knew exactly what she was up to.

First stop was Mrs. Cora Hardacre, who taught the class which maintained The Nest. The classroom wasn't what she expected. There was a wall of six computers and the bulk of the rest of the room was taken up with a couple of couches and work tables. The other three walls were covered with bulletin boards and pictures. Already, a couple of students had set up for the morning.

Mrs. Hardacre sat behind her desk but stood up quickly when Rosella walked over. "Can I help you?"

Rosella handed her a card. "Dr. Rosella Tassoni. The FBI called me in to investigate the murders."

"It's so tragic."

"You teach the advanced programming classes as well as being the faculty advisor for the yearbook?"

"I do. I've been here for seven years now."

Rosella made a few notes in a notepad. "What can you tell me about The Nest?"

"It started as a social experiment my class suggested a few years ago. I thought it was a fun way for them to learn programming. It lets the school connect in different ways." Mrs. Hardacre pulled up the website on one of the computers.

"What do the students do today to maintain it?"

"They are the site administrators. Of course, the school board and the administration have a look, in case of cyberbullying, and the school puts closure announcements there. But they leave the maintenance to the students in my class."

"Would you mind if I spoke with them this morning? I understand they meet first period."

"They do, though most are in here off and on all day. I have an open door policy."

"Good to know. I'm also going to need a roster."

By then, more students had filed in and Rosella took a seat on one of the couches, surprised at how comfortable it felt. The bell rang and she noticed it was a smaller class, fifteen students. Sipping on her tea, she watched them as they settled in for their first period.

"Good morning class. We have a special guest with us today. Dr. Rosella Tassoni is with the FBI—"

"You're covering the murder, aren't you?"

"Can you find who did it?"

"Do you work with the FBI a lot?"

"What's it like?"

The questions came rapid fire and before Rosella could speak, Mrs. Hardacre held up her hands. "*Enough*, class. Dr. Tassoni is going to speak with you all for a bit today. If she is not speaking with you, I want you checking over anything that may need your attention. Don't forget, you all need to come up with your semester project idea by the end of the month."

With that, she took a seat at her desk and Rosella stood up and looked over the group.

"My name is Dr. Rosella Tassoni and I'm a Forensic Mythologist."

"Is that really a thing?"

"I'm working on it. Forensic anthropology wasn't a thing until the thirties, or established until the seventies. " Rosella chose to ignore the question. She was really tired of it. Someday she'd get to the point where she never hear it again. Then she'd know hearing it so often was worth it.

That day couldn't come soon enough.

"Some evidence came to my attention when I arrived in town yesterday that one of the victims found a certain game on The Nest."

"You're talking about the Midnight Game," a girl said from behind her Mac.

"I am."

"That group?" Another student turned around their laptop and Rosella looked at the group.

"So it's a group?" Rosella made a note: *the group currently consisted of over 200 of the almost 1000 students in the school*. "Let me see that a second."

Rosella quickly skimmed the page looking at recent posts. Aesthetically, the site looked like a mix of the old MySpace with the newer features of Facebook. But instead of the traditional Facebook blue, it had the school colors of emerald green and gold.

The badly pixelated picture looked like someone had either stolen it off of Deviantart, or tried to make something on their own in Photoshop without having any idea what they were doing. She was leaning towards the latter, considering the art looked as if its artist attempted to do a subtly smoky background. But, instead, they smeared grey all over the screen. A candle, badly isolated from its original image, was the only object. It announced The Midnight Game in a font she supposed was chosen to appear "creepy."

She stared at the posts.

Can't wait 2 play.

Last weekend was a thrill!

Home alone this weekend...let the game begin!

Does it matter if you use a scented candle?

Posts continued on in a similar fashion but what really stood out to Rosella was that students were going to play *again* tomorrow night. "Is there a way to see who started this? Mrs. Hardacre, may I recruit one of your students?"

"Of course, Dr. Tassoni."

"What's your doctorate in?" A guy asked from the back of the room.

"Anthropology. I did my dissertation on Forensic Mythology." Rosella felt like she was being interviewed, and the feeling she'd had a couple days before came back. This was why she only lectured to senior college students. She pointed at the guy who showed her the group along with the girl who mentioned it. 'What are your names?"

"Micheal Klam."

"Charity Jenas."

Rosella nodded and handed each of them a card. "You two are in charge of monitoring the group's activity. If anything suspicious comes up, call me. Find out who started this group."

Both nodded.

"Now, tell me about the site."

For the half hour she let the students show her around The Nest. They set her up with a guest profile. As the class dismissed, Rosella picked up her bag and made a few last notes. "Thank you, Mrs. Hardacre."

"Let me know if I can help in any way."

Rosella made her way through the throng of students looking around and figuring out her next steps. Band practice and football practice were both after school. Shay had had a theater class this next period and Ashley used her free period for SGA meetings later in the day. Maybe by walking through their last day, she could get some insight as to why these five students were the ones who didn't live to see another sunrise. This was the one place all five had in common.

She had her work cut out for her. Because the group was playing again tomorrow night.

And her killer might strike again.

Rosella counted her blessings, for what had to be the twentieth time that day, and thanked the Good Lord that she was no longer in high school as she made her way out at the end of the day. It

41

had been seven hours of teenaged drama and constant questions of Rosella's abilities.

And she still had to go back to the station and conduct interviews.

"Siri, get me directions to nearest place that serves tea." Rosella spoke into her phone, craving some caffeine and atomic amounts of sugar as well as wanting to follow up on another lead. "Make it one with a high number of check-ins."

She had barely left the parking lot when her phone rang.

"Dr. Tassoni."

"Petalo."

"Ciao, papa." Rosella smiled. "Has Mama calmed down from yesterday?"

"She's still upset with you, Petalo."

"I worked hard to get where I am." Rosella sighed.

"Did you really show her a memorial for the victims? She looked up the case you're on."

"She was getting on my case *for* taking the case, papa. We both know you can handle the wedding without me."

"How is *this* case going?"

"I remembered why I was so happy to graduate high school."

That comment earned her a laugh. "Be careful up there, Petalo. We'll see you when you get back."

"Think Mama will calm down before then?"

"Your guess is as good as mine. I've got to get back in the kitchen. Ciao, Petalo."

"Ciao, papa." Rosella hung up the phone, glad at least one of her parents was on her side. Honestly, she wasn't sure she'd ever win her mother over to her idea of what she wanted to do with her life.

Sense and Sensibiliteas was rumored to be one of the top hang out spots for the students of Huntington Prep. She'd heard it mentioned a couple of times during her visit to the school. It also didn't hurt that it was a tea shop and she was desperately in need of some hot tea.

She lucked into a space in the little lot beside it as someone pulled out as she was pulling in. Stepping into the shop she couldn't help but smile at the coffee shop atmosphere. Some local radio station was playing lightly in the background as almost every table in the place was full of students doing homework or just goofing off on laptops.

A couple waved to her as she made her way to the counter and she smiled and waved back before looking at the menu.

She loved options. White, black, chai, green, herbal and so many combinations of all of the above.

"Welcome to Sense and Sensibiliteas." A middle aged man smiled at her from behind the counter. "You must be that myth lady they've all been talking about."

"Dr. Rosella Tassoni." She smiled, shaking the hand he offered her.

"Franco Toffler."

"Toffler…" The name was familiar.

"My son, Orlando is on the football team. He was friends with Sam." The man let out a sigh. "This has been hard on him. Orlando is a good kid though. He comes in after games and does inventory and has been helping me with the books."

Rosella nodded making a note about that. "I'm sorry for your son's loss."

"As am I, Dr. Tassoni. What will it be today?"

"What do you recommend?"

"Considering you look like you are in serious need of caffiene—"

"You have no idea." Rosella bit back a snort.

Franco chuckled. "Sounds like you need The Katherine. More jitters than a gothic heroine."

"Someone's really into Jane Austen."

"My wife."

Rosella laughed, Mom and Pop shops were the best. "What's in The Katherine?"

"A black tea blend with lychee and mango."

"Sounds fantastic." She handed him her card. "Give me the biggest size you have."

Rosella wasn't sure what it said about American society that they placed such an emphasis on sports but she eyed the clock waiting for football practice to end so that she could interview some of the players about Sam Watts' death. One would think a murder investigation would take precedence but no, there was a big game Friday night and the team need to work through Watts' death.

With a huff, she made her way to the lobby to collect her first person. "Ted Downer?"

A kid, who stood a half foot taller than Rosella, stood up. "Ma'am?"

A pair of adults stood up beside him and Rosella held out her hand. "You must be Ted's parents. I'm Dr. Rosella Tassoni, the Forensic Mythologist and FBI consultant. I have a few questions for Ted about Sam Watts."

"Forensic Mythologist?"

"You'd be surprised how often I get cases. Now if you don't mind, follow me."

Rosella led them through the bullpen, toward her "office." She shook her head at the nameplate she found on the door. The flowers on the plate's border were a nice touch, and the writing let her know that some officer's little girl had had fun making it for her. It let the entire station know this was *Dr. Rosella's Office*. Though she wasn't sure how the little girl had known she loved violets.

"Have a seat." She nodded to a seat and sat down on the opposite side of the table. His parents sat on either side. "So you've been friends with Sam for most of your lives?"

"Yeah, we grew up together, played little league together. We were talking about getting on the same college team, Ohio State maybe." Ted swallowed hard and Rosella gave him a second. "I can't believe…he missed practice Saturday and I knew something was wrong cause he was at the game the night before."

"You won, right?"

"Yeah, he caught the winning pass. We got shakes at Big Kahuna after the game and he headed home."

"Did he say anything about playing a game?"

"He showed me some page on the site. But who wants to wander around the house for hours in the dark?"

"I ask myself that question all the time." Rosella smirked. "He was a part of the group?"

"Yeah, I guess."

"What group?"

Rosella looked up from her notes at Mr. Downer. "We received evidence that all five victims were a part of a group called 'The Midnight Game' where they were playing a game supposedly based on an ancient pagan ritual."

Ted's mother looked at her son. "Were you playing this game over at Ivan's?"

Ted frantically shook his head. "No, mom, we played video games before catching a couple hours sleep before practice."

Rosella made note of the alibi. "How about any of the other victims?"

"What about them?"

"Did you know any of them?"

"Sure, half the team knows Ashley. She was dating Toffler."

"Toffler?" Rosella had heard that name somewhere before. Scanning through her notes, she spotted the name. "You mean Orlando Toffler, he's second string, right? His parents own that tea shop."

"Was. Rumor has it he's going to get Sam's spot next season now."

Rosella made a note of it. "Well, thank you for your help. Can you send Toffler in?"

"Sure thing, Dr. Tassoni." Ted held out his hand. "It was a pleasure to meet you."

"You as well." Rosella smiled.

It was a few minutes until a guy just over six foot came walking in the room, the bags under his eyes telling Rosella that he'd had a rather long week. "Orlando Toffler?"

"You're that expert the FBI called in."

"Dr. Rosella Tassoni. I'm a Forensic Mythologist."

"That's a thing?" He took a seat after shaking her hand.

"Technically, I'm a forensic anthropologist. I'm working on the other one." She sat down. "I hear you have a connection to two of the victims."

"Yeah. Ashely, she was…we'd been together for over a year. I…she was at the game and we went out after and she wanted to get home early, something about a game."

Rosella nodded. "The ritual starts at midnight."

"Right. Anyways, I went to the shop—"

"Sense and Sensabiliteas? I was in there earlier. Your dad seems nice."

"Yeah. I help him with the books and I do some of the blending of tea for the weekend after the games on Friday nights when we play at home. With practice I can't work a lot during the week so I do some hours then. Sleep a few

47

hours and close the store on Saturday. Next thing I know the cops are knocking on my door asking questions because Ashley had been found."

"Have you been having any trouble in your relationship, lately?"

He shook his head.

"What about Sam Watts?"

"We've been playing together since we were little. He's closer to the right size for the position. We're pretty evenly matched, skill-wise."

Rosella jotted down some notes. "I'm sorry for your loss."

"Thanks." Orlando nodded.

"So what happens now? Sam Watts is dead, you get first string?"

Orlando shrugged. "I guess? Not the way I would have wanted it. I'd rather earn it."

"Fair enough. Do you guys have security recordings of the store between 12 and 3:30 that morning?"

"I'll have to ask Dad but we should still have the footage."

"Thank you for your time."

"You asked to see me, Dr. Tassoni?"

Rosella looked up to see a group of kids standing in the doorway. Right. Remind me of who's who again?"

The girl who took a seat directly across from her held out her hand. "Kristin Wickens."

Taking a look at her notes, she nodded. "Right, you are in the class with Michael and

Charity and you were in drama with Shay Hanley."

"Yes, I do the groups, like the Midnight Game. I authorized it to go live on the site."

"Is there a process you use to determine what goes live and what doesn't?" Rosella asked as the others took a seat.

"It was a game. There are dozens like it on the site. I looked it up on the Creepypasta Wikia and while it seemed dumb, I saw no harm in it." She fidgeted in her seat.

"And why didn't you take it down after the murders?" To Rosella, this went hand in hand with the group who was willing to play the other night. Why would you play a game that got five people killed the week before? And why didn't the site administrators do anything about it?

"To me, it would make me look suspicious. Anyone in the drama department knew that I had originally auditioned for Shay's part and that I was in charge of groups, in fact, people tend to let me know in the hallway if they want to add new ones. It would lead a path to me. I figured people wouldn't be dumb enough to play it after what happened…"

"I thought so too. Thank you, Miss Wickens." She turned to the person on the left. "Frank Strakr, thanks for coming back in. I know we talked the other day but you are in the class…"

"Are we all suspects or something?"

"You all have administrative access to the site where my UnSub is getting his or her victim pool. Forgive me for being thorough and trying to save the lives of your remaining classmates—any more questions?"

A silent group of five met her. "Mr. Strakr, what do you do for the site?"

"I manage new accounts. This is my busiest time of year, making sure all the freshman have an account. I was in the original class and loved it so much that I took it three years in a row."

"One of the youngest to take the advance programming class. Not too different from you. I looked you up after you came to our class that day. You were a bit of a prodigy back in the day."

Rosella couldn't help but be a little impressed that one of these kids bothered to do some research, though the way he said back in the day bothered her. She wasn't *that* old...

"So you know quite a lot about me."

"Half the town does, doesn't mean I did it."

"Perhaps." She turned to the person on his left. "And you are?"

"Charlene Major. I work tech support with Michael."

Rosella made a note. "That means you have access to tracking information."

"But so does the whole class, and the administration for that matter."

"Charlene, you help Miss Wickens?"

"Yeah, it's a large job. And to back her up, we talked about taking down the site, but also it's their first amendment rights to assemble and talk about the game."

"You realize, if the murders continue, you could be indicted for any number of accessory charges? Top of your class in Civics, then?"

Like a true politician, she avoided the first question. "I want to work in Washington, someday." But it was only a fent. "You realize, of course, that the site is protected under safe harbor laws. Like how Google can link you to something illegal, or Facebook can host groups planning illegal things. The host isn't culpable."

Rosella grunted. "Start apartment shopping, now. It's a bear, trust me." Rosella turned to the person on Miss Wickens right. "Toby Mortensen? You were in SGA with Ashley. What's happening to her position as treasurer?"

"For now, I'm taking it over as well as my duties as Vice President. Once the investigation is concluded, we'll hold a special election and elect her replacement."

"Any favorites for the race?"

"Nora Browning ran against her last semester. I wouldn't be surprised to see her try again."

"Why did Ashley win?"

"She was someone who reached out. She volunteered, and actually meant what she said. Nothing against Nora, but there was less evidence that she meant what she said, you know?"

"Jillian Miles? You played saxophone with Edwin, right?"

"Yeah, he was first chair and I was second, but that's not enough motive to kill him."

"I didn't say it was." Rosella stared at the group. "I've got a few more questions for all of you. Starting with, where were you both Friday nights between the hours of midnight and 3:33 AM?"

The bullpen was silent as the sun went down the next night. Rosella's fears had been confirmed and a group of students were going to play the game tonight.

And with all the publicity this case was getting, Rosella was sure her killer would be out on the prowl.

"The Midnight Game, and the subsequent murders, lead the FBI and me to believe that our UnSub is a man. That being said, we do not know who is a potential target. He is not following the Midnight Game lore. Last weekend the victims did not have a history of being troublemakers. Quite the opposite actually. We do not know how many they are going to try for, *if* they try."

She studied the group of officers who were getting ready to go out and patrol. "Keep an eye out for anything suspicious. You have all been given files with details of the creepypasta lore. The problem is, there is nothing in the lore to really describe the Midnight Man. The closest we get is a vague description that his shadow is darker than midnight itself."

Nods filled the room and Rosella let out a sigh. "If he stays with the lore, our UnSub will not strike until after midnight. But after that, the clock starts. At least a hundred students are playing. So concentrate your search in residential areas."

Leaving the bullpen, she made her way to the break room where Michael and Charity had agreed to help monitor The Nest.

All that was left was to wait.

Rosella took another sip of tea while going over the ME's reports. It was quarter to midnight and she was somewhere between exhausted and wired. She blamed The Katherine. Soft music held sway in her conference room, but clicking was all she could hear from across the hall.

The Suspect Wall had almost twenty photos pinned-up, making it far too complicated for her liking. The problem was this site was open to over one thousand students, faculty, staff, and to some extent parents and the public as a whole. Anyone could know who was playing and some of the kids even geotagged their homes, which made it easier for things like this to happen.

Add to that, this so-called Midnight Man was supposedly nothing more than a shadow himself, blending in with the darkness of the night.

Granted, if the murders still happened she could personally take at least two down: she had an officer monitoring Charity and Michael through the night. Every little step helped, that was for sure. The rest of the computer class were at Huntington Prep, confined to their classroom as an organized sleepover. She hated to do that. The police department had unhappy parents on their hands, but these students were the ones with the most access to the site, and she needed to eliminate them.

Charity stuck her head in the door. "They're going to go offline in about ten minutes. We'll have no way to monitor the game."

"Is there a way to monitor site traffic during the game? That way, if someone cheats and goes online, we can know?"

"I'm working on it." Michael yelled from across the room.

Rosella eyed the clock. "Just hurry. The game's about to start."

"We know."

Rosella turned back to her files, making notes on her computer and trying to figure out how this string of seemingly random pieces fit together.

"Did we figure out who started the group?"

"I'm working on that." Charity glanced at the photos of her and Michael on the wall, among the other possible suspects. "Not going to lie, that's a little unsettling."

"Just doing my job." Rosella shrugged.

"Doesn't make it less unsettling."

"If it makes you feel better, if you two haven't left this station between now and 3:33three A.M., then I get to be your alibi."

Charity paused a second to consider it. "That does help."

With that, Charity made her way across the hall to her corner and Rosella turned to her wall of suspects. She needed to narrow down this list because, right now, she didn't have a lot to go on.

A piano arrangement of "I Wanna Be Like You" filled the room as she looked between her notes. Half were already put in her computer, but the other half were scattered among the pads she laid all over the table. Each case was a puzzle; she had some of the pieces for this one. But it was like she had all of the middle ones and none of the edges to help her makes sense of it all.

This had always been her least favorite part.

Then there were the organs. They had long since left the period of viability and she hadn't gotten reports of anyone suddenly dropping off the transplant list, or any matching organs seized off the black market. Regardless, she couldn't completely rule out the black market. Especially this far out.

For not the first time, she wished they hadn't waited almost a week to call her in. Granted, the FBI didn't get called in until Monday, but even then that would have given her a few more viable leads to chase. Some leads faded away the longer she didn't have access to them.

The black market wasn't her only option. The UnSub could be doing other things with them. She would prefer to not have to think about some of the options, but they were still options. He could just be taking them intentionally to throw her off. Let her chase the invisible trail of non-existent organs.

"Gina?" Rosella stuck her head out of the office.

"She got called away. Something about a bonfire off our Route 311."

"Aren't you in the middle of a burn ban?"

"We are." The officer nodded.

"Tell her to come see me when she gets back." Rosella went back into her office just as the clock made a chiming sound. Just like Cinderella at the ball, she was out of time.

The game had begun.

Matches lay sporadically across the floor. Either the Midnight Man had almost caught sixteen-year-old Tameka Conrad, or she had trouble lighting her candle in time. Either way, she felt that there were more matches on the floor around this home than there had been at Ashley's.

Tameka's body lay in the bathroom, tangled in the shower curtain, different from the first five victims. She certainly struggled. But the results were the same.

The body laid over the side of the tub, almost bent in half, a gaping wound in the abdomen and no signs of any of her internal organs. The candle lay amongst its shattered glass, inside the tub. A blackened wick was beside her face.

Rosella found the piece of paper, complete with blood, a bag of cheese doodles (the rules never said you couldn't snack), and notes from the creepypasta. At least this one had done her research.

Continuing to walk the house, she paused for a second to watch the sun come up, and hoped that there weren't five more bodies waiting to be discovered.

Her gut told her she wasn't going to be that lucky.

"What do we know about the victim?" Rosella put her focus back into profiling hoping that it would relieve the headache she felt coming on.

"Tameka Conrad. Sophomore, same school as the others. Adopted by the Conrads when she was eight. Been in and out of trouble with both the school and the law the last year or so."

Rosella looked up quickly from her notes at the slight change in M.O. This was closer to the source material, as if between weeks, the UnSub looked closer into the myth.

But why would he suddenly care about the creepypasta text?

"Interesting. And her parents found her?"

"They're out front. We asked them to stay around in case you had questions for them."

Rosella nodded and went out to find a distraught couple standing on the front walk with a couple of officers. She took her time approaching, so she could study them. Both were in their late forties and Mrs. Conrad's face had mascara tracks running with her tears. Her husband held her close, his own tears flowing freely as they stared at the house.

"Mr. And Mrs. Conrad?"

They nodded.

"I'm Dr. Rosella Tassoni, the FBI called me in to assist with the case. I'm sorry for your loss." She handed her card to Mr. Conrad who stuck it in his pocket. "I'm sorry to ask this right now but it might help me help the FBI bring your daughter's killer to justice."

"Anything. Meka was our world." Mrs. Conrad grabbed a tissue out of her pocket. "We just, it was our anniversary so we left overnight to celebrate. She's sixteen, she should have been fine."

Rosella tried to comfort the grieving woman but to be honest, she was at a bit of a lost herself. How could these kids play this game knowing what happened to their classmates the week before? She knew some did it for the thrill. After all, what reason was there to roam a pitch black house at odd hours of the night? And the added thrill of there being a murderer out and about...

"But after her classmates died—" Mrs. Conrad broke into another sob and her husband pulled her close.

"You said you had a question for us, Dr. Tassoni?"

"I heard that Tomeka had been in trouble a few times in the last year."

Mr. Conrad nodded. "She's been acting out. Normal teenager stuff. The last couple of months, she started to get her act together again."

"So she's been better?" Rosella noted. "What kind of punishments did she get?"

"Why is this relevant?"

Rosella let out a sigh. "I have a running theory, to be honest."

"The cops let her off with a warning. But she was in and out of detention a fair bit."

Making a note in her notepad, Rosella looked back at the house where she could see them about to wheel out Tomeka's body. "I'm sorry for your loss. I'll be in touch, but if you think of something or notice something out of place, please let us know."

"Of course."

Rosella nodded to Dr. Crowdell who followed his technicians out of the house. "Let me know if anything changes from last week to today."

"You think it might?"

"Honestly? I'm not sure. The M.O. might have changed. I'm curious if something else changed too."

"I'll let you know." He nodded to the technicians who loaded the body in into the back of the van. "This needs to end."

"I'm hoping we're not just beginning."

"Do you really think we'll be that lucky?"

Rosella eyed the medical examiner.

"I find with cases like this, you rarely are."

Wandering back into the house, Rosella walked it one last time, taking in the matches and realizing that Tomeka had probably made it through a good chunk of the three and a half hours of the game.

"She was one of the last to die tonight."

"Dr. Tassoni?" An officer stuck his head into the room she was in. "Reports of another body just came through."

Making her way out to her car, she bit back a groan when she saw that the press had gotten wind that this crime scene was related to the ones from the previous week.

"Dr. Tassoni, is it true that there are no leads?"

"Is this the work of the Friday Fiend?"

"What is being done to keep the children of Huntington safe?"

Her headache was officially back.

There was something weird about this second round of victims. Rachmaninoff played as she hung five new pictures next to the ones that had been staring at her. But they were different from the first five and she couldn't help but wonder *why* the difference. Why had the UnSub seemingly spent longer with each victim— making it much more efficient, much more like the myth he was hiding behind.

She hated when they started to get cocky and showed off. But something about the first five victims seemed different besides. She had nothing solid to base it on, yet, but she had this feeling in her gut that the key was hiding here.

"Why change this time around?" Agent Wednesday eyed the board.

"Several factors maybe. It could be you, it could be me, it could be both, or it could be the media attention. Chances are it's a combination of all of the above. Our UnSub must have found he liked the attention."

"Great, an egomaniac." Agent Pugsley let out a sigh. "Just what we needed."

Rosella turned back to staring at the wall of victims and she heard the agents leave. Agent

Pugsley was right; if their killer was starting to do this to stoke his own ego, then they were in trouble. As long as he had a reason to do what he was doing, as nonsensical a reason it might be, there was a pattern that eventually might be able to lead them to their UnSub. If he started acting out because he liked the attention, then he might become erratic and Rosella would prefer him not becoming *less* predictable.

Her phone rang and she turned to see that it was the realtor she'd been talking to in DC. "Dr. Tassoni."

"Dr. Tassoni, this is Debra Saunders."

"Sorry about cancelling our appointment, I was called in on a case."

"I sent you an email this morning, hopefully it will still be on the market when you make it back to DC but I think it's perfect."

Sitting down in the chair, Rosella logged into her email and found pictures of the house in question. Eyeing the price, she felt her eyebrow shoot up. "And within my price range. That *is* cute."

"Let me know when you're back in town and if it hasn't gone off the market, we'll take a look."

"Will do. Thanks, Mrs. Saunders." Rosella hung up and eyed the photos again, wondering if she was doing the right thing by moving to the DC area. For one thing, she was doing pretty well for herself, being willing to go from place to place, not that she *wouldn't* once she had a home base.

But back to New York and the ten victims. Dr. Crowdell would be busy for a while with all the bodies but she wasn't expecting anything new, maybe a change in the drugs, but that depended on the UnSub's mood.

Part of her problem is she couldn't see what possessed him to do the first round, much less the second.

It was a somber crowd that gathered outside of Huntington Prep as the sun set. Speakers had been set up and Rosella wasn't completely surprised to hear hymns. A beautiful orchestral arrangement—Kreisler's arrangement? Rosella tried to place its composer—seemed to soothe the crowd. Principal Gutenberg made his way to the makeshift stage.

Rosella circled the crowd, studying the mourning faces. Across the way, she could see Agents Wednesday and Pugsley doing the same.

Eventually, at least Rosella assumed, criminals would figure out that this *CSI* obsessed culture would catch onto their tricks. But still, the odds were that her UnSub was here, somewhere.

Pictures of the ten victims could be seen on the stage and the memorial provided a backdrop to the fake stage as Gutenberg began speaking, welcoming everyone to the vigil. Flashes came from where the press were trying to capture every minute of the event.

"Our school has been hit hard by the events of the last couple of weeks, but still, we stand strong. On behalf of Huntington Prep and the community, I want to thank our police force, the FBI, and Dr. Rosella Tassoni for their efforts in trying to bring this killer to justice."

Rosella pasted a smile on her face, internally screaming at the man for mentioning her and bringing her presence at the event to a spotlight. But she waved as people around her thanked her and the applause continued for a few more seconds. She moved through the crowd, watching faces, reading body language, and making note of suspicious actions. There were a couple of parents lingering near their children. Charlene Major stood alone, pale, and tense. Orlando Toffler was surrounded by the football team, in mutual support. Rosella was not surprised to see the shallowness of some students: a group of girls were in the back, by the press, just there to be seen.

The choir assembled on stage and performed an eight part harmony as they sang. She had to note that events like this brought a community together and it encouraged her. But to help them get to there, she had to bring them some closure.

Pulling out her notepad, she made some more observations as she continued to circle the crowd. The mayor made a speech, as well as some teachers, friends of the victims, family members all the while taking notes. Some of these would go to the FBI, some she would investigate herself.

About halfway through the service, candlelight started to fill the front lawn of the school as everyone took a candle. A ritual to pay respects to the victims of another ritual. She wasn't sure if that was ironic or not. But the sentiment was there, and the respect.

"Dr. Tassoni?"

Rosella turned to see Principal Gutenberg looking at her along with a good chunk of the crowd. She realized he must have called her name a couple of times but she had been so lost in her thoughts that she hadn't heard him. Reluctantly, she made her way to the stage. "You'll have to forgive me, Principal Gutenberg, I was lost in my thoughts and didn't hear what you said previously."

"People were asking about the myth."

Rosella took the microphone, in her element for a second. "The Midnight Game is fauxlore—literally, artificial folklore—started and spread online as a 'pagan' ritual to punish rule breakers. It's the Millenials' Bloody Mary and Light as a Feather, Stiff as a Board. Over the years it has gained notoriety, and evolved into the game that the kids on The Nest were playing. After performing the summoning ritual, the player then wanders around the dark house with nothing more than a candle and salt for just over three and a half hours."

"Why would someone do that?" A parent asked from about a fourth of the way through the crowd.

"Your guess is as good as mine. Most websites say that it's a good game for adrenaline junkies." Rosella smiled at getting a question. One might argue about giving away this much information about an ongoing investigation but was she really saying anything they couldn't find if they'd bothered to go on creepypasta websites?

"What's the point?" Another person asked.

"The point is to not get caught. If you can make it from midnight to 3:33 A.M., then you have won the game."

"And we've seen what happens when you get caught?"

"Online, there are no recorded cases—before this one—of someone getting caught by the Midnight Man. Though, like our friends on the web, I don't believe that these children summoned a *preternatural* killer. It is an actual person who is trying to hide behind the myth."

"Which is what you specialize in?"

She nodded at the statement. "Yes. I want to thank you all for being so welcoming and helpful with mine and the FBI's investigation."

Nodding to the memorial behind her, she turned back to the crowd. "They are why I do what I do. If I can bring peace to even one family, then it is all worth it. I spent years studying myths and their origins and it still amazes me how people abuse them. But I will do my best to bring the person who did this to your children, classmates, friends, siblings to justice."

That earned her applause and she made her way off the stage and headed for the back of the crowd.

"Where's that myth lady?"

Rosella looked up from her file at the sound of a woman's screech. Mentally reviewing the last twenty-four hours, she tried to remember what she might have done to upset a woman. Nothing came to mind.

Taking a deep breath, she made her way to the doorway to find a group of parents being held back by some officers. "Is there a problem?"

"You talked to my daughter. You talked to all of our kids."

"I believe I talked to some of you as well. But any kids under the age of eighteen had a parent with them. If you were not with your daughter, then she was a legal adult and I was well within my rights to question her." Rosella tried to place the mom to the kid.

"I don't want some murder investigation messing with her head. Scouts are looking at her for a scholarship and if you mess her up here in the beginning of the season..."

One thing Rosella absolutely hated when she got stuck in a case that involved high schoolers were overzealous sports parents. Well, she hated many things, but that ranked pretty high on the list. So to have this soccer mom stand in front of her...she bit back the condescending tone she so desperately wanted to use.

"Who is your daughter?"

"Bailey Maidwell."

Rosella flipped through the pages and found notes. Bailey was in the class that ran the site and she had talked to her about different features on the site. Nothing traumatic. "We discussed The Nest, according to my notes. I asked her if she wanted a parent present."

"She's still in school."

"She's over eighteen." Rosella nodded. "Some of you were with your children when I talked to them." She pointed to the board where the ten photos hung. "Those children, *your* children's classmates, deserve justice. And I'm not going to let some overzealous soccer moms tell me and the FBI that we can't investigate for fear of a scholarship."

The police had tried their best to keep the nature of the murders away from the general public. The papers and local TV stations were running old prom pictures or pictures taken on summer vacation and crime scene photos, but none of the bodies. None of the pictures the news ran showed Ashley's body, in a heap on the living room floor, in of a pool of her own blood or Sam Watts on the kitchen floor, a snack in his cold hand. There was a reason that these pictures weren't out, but if she had to use them to get the attention of these parents she would.

Rosella watched as the group of irate parents got a look at just how sick a person that Rosella was having to deal with. Mrs. Maidwell's face had lost all of its color, her hand brought to her mouth trying to cover up her shock.

Out of the whole group, though, none of their faces screamed anything more than parents concerned for their kids.

Ready to get back to work, she headed back for her conference room. There was little a parent like that wouldn't do to protect their kids. In fact, she had investigated that lead and was still waiting on alibis. After all, with talent scouts and whatnot it was all about being noticed.

The day's paper sat on the desk and Rosella looked at herself at herself attending the vigil. She really wished she was as confident about this case as the paper made her out to be.

Angry parents gone, Rosella settled back down to her computer to find another email from her realtor.

Thought you might like this one as well. Let me know! ~Deb

Clicking on the listing link, Rosella looked at the three bedroom home. She knew she wanted three at minimum and this one seemed nice. She'd have to add it to the list with the other one. Grabbing her *Moving* notepad, she made a note about the property and did a quick check on commercial properties inside DC.

Satisfied, she turned back to the case at hand and wondered when Dr. Crowdell would have the results of the newest autopsies. Ten victims in a week's time. This UnSub didn't waste time and Rosella couldn't help but note that some part of her was worried that he would escalate again

Grabbing the file on the newest victims, she studied their supposed crimes and wondered how they connected. Sure, all five were in The Nest group, but so were almost a hundred other students. Some of the others had to be rule breakers, too.

So why those five?

Why the first five, for that matter? Rosella couldn't figure out what had made him select them. There were around two hundred kids in that group. Take away the ones who didn't play, and thus got themselves virtually disqualified from being killed, why those five? What made her UnSub select them? And why switch for the second set?

"Dr. Tassoni?"

Rosella turned to see Dr. Crowdell standing in the doorway,

"What do you have for me?"

"After comparing the wounds of the first five victims with the latest group, I have a guess as to what our murder weapon is."

"What is it?"

Dr. Crowdell handed her a file and she opened it to find his preliminary report. "It's some form of a knife. The blade is four to six inches long and less than two inches wide. I also think there are a couple knives involved since some of the wounds appear different yet stay consistent to knife wounds."

Rosella looked at the file flipping through his findings. "I'll ask around, this could be where he decided to mix various lore together."

"It is a good thing they called you in, isn't it?"

She shrugged. "Similar results on the last five?"

He nodded. "I plan on having my full report for you tomorrow."

"I might stop by and examine the bodies tomorrow as well."

"Feel free. As I said when you came before, I want to help where I can."

He left her conference room and Rosella examined the file some more. There were many ceremonial knives that one could use for something like this. Narrowing it down might take some time. But why use a ceremonial dagger, that is if her hunch was correct? Either they really got off on these killings or their ego was already healthy when they got started. Maybe a bit of both, but she didn't like what that meant.

The UnSub wasn't going to stop until they were caught.

The sun was setting when Rosella finally stepped out of the police station. To her dismay, there were still a few members of the press, including one face she'd been desperately hoping wouldn't make an appearance.

"Dr. Tassoni, a word?" Bridgett Rosso held up her phone.

"That's funny." Rosella couldn't help but chuckle. "After what you said about me after the case in Phoenix—you really think I'd give you anything?"

"Rosella, darling, it was only good journalism."

Rosella scoffed. "It was borderline slander. How you're still allowed to publish anything in that rag—"

"I'm actually freelancing now."

"Oh, really now?" Rosella walked past her. "There have been children who died here, Bridgett. There are parents who lost their children. None of them deserve you sensationalizing this story and selling it to highest bidder."

"People want to know about the Friday Fiend. I coined the name, keep that in mind."

Rosella stopped and took a deep breath. "We both know that I'm not going to tell you anything that I haven't already said to the press. I wouldn't before Phoenix and I definitely won't now. Good luck on your story, or true crime novel, or whatever you're doing, Bridgett."

Heading for her car, she dug her phone out of her bag to call home. After a few rings, someone picked up and she could hear the familiar sounds of the kitchen in the background. "Petalla, how is your case?"

"Ciao, Papa." Rosella smiled, breathing a quiet sigh of relief that it wasn't her mother that picked up. "It's not going a whole lot."

"I saw where there are more victims. You made quite a statement last night. Your mother and I were proud of you."

"Is that Rosella?" Her mother's voice could be heard in the background and after the slight sound of a scuffle, her mom's voice became dominant. "Rosella, how's New York? We saw you on the news and Viola was on the phone in a minute telling us how brave you were. But we miss you here, it's not the same without you."

"Mom, I'm thirty-two and it's time for me to move on, to do this for a living."

A sigh came across the phone. "When did my baby girl grow up?"

"Around the time she got a PhD."

"That doesn't mean I want you to move half-way across the country."

"Mama, we've been over this." Rosella bit back anything else that she wanted to say. "I'm moving where the work is. I'll get more cases if I'm located near Langley and Quantico."

"Give the girl a break, dear." Her father's voice came in the background. "At least she calls when she's out of town, unlike that brother of hers."

"How is the case, dear?" Her mother changed the subject. "I heard there were more victims."

"There are, and I don't like some of the things I see in this case. Hopefully, we can stop him before next Friday…"

"You can do it, Petalla." Her father must have taken the phone.

"Get some rest." Her mother's voice could be heard loud and clear. "You looked tired on that press conference."

"It wasn't a press conference." Rosella didn't bother to hold in a groan at that. "It was a vigil where I found my soapbox."

"Ignore your mother, you looked fine." Her father had the tone where he was humoring her mother and Rosella bit back a giggle. "But get some rest."

"I will, Papa."

She was officially tired of this conference room.

No matter how she moved the pictures around or what music she put on, the walls of this station seemed to close in on her. What was worse is she felt like she had done absolutely nothing to eliminate suspects.

Charity and Michael had eliminated themselves as suspects when they were in the station for the entire three and a half hours, along with the rest of their class and the teacher. That meant the entire site's administration was innocent—removing the possibility it was an inside job.

After all, high schoolers were petty. There were people who got ahead because of these murders but Rosella had to honestly ask herself if any of them were worth it. Then again, some of her friends at Quantico often said that *the crime didn't have to make sense to anyone but the UnSub.*

She'd talked to a couple dozen people and some alibis checked out. Others weren't airtight so she kept them in the maybe pile. After all, while Netflix could say that you were watching *Supernatural* at odd hours of the night (not an activity Rosella recommended)—that still left you a window. Netflix's server couldn't tell Rosella that they were actually in front of the screen through the binge.

Rosella got up with a sigh and made herself another cup of tea, noting that she'd have to either send someone to Sense and Sensabiliteas or get some more tea for herself soon.

Maybe she should cut back on the caffeine.

Rosella stormed into the FBI's conference room and saw that they were no better off than her. "You mean to tell me that this police force doubled patrols through the area in question and no one saw anything? Five people were killed in the space of three hours and no one saw anything suspicious?"

Agents Wednesday looked at her. "What do you want us to tell you. The UnSub managed to get in and out unseen. Our superiors about ready to call in the BAU."

"Because this guy needs more media attention." Rosella let out a sigh.

"The only description we got was a black figure. Officer Branden Prynne saw one about 1:30 that morning and followed him but lost him when he cut through some woods. All black, wearing a ski mask, with a knife hanging by his side."

"You didn't think to tell me this?"

"With all due respect—"

She waved him off, and addressed the bullpen. "Officer Prynne, if you are out here, please report to my conference room in five."

Agent Pugsley pulled her out of her thoughts. "So what is this Midnight Man supposed to look like?"

"A shadow. Remember, our gamers are wandering a pitch black house. There are several signs that he is nearby. Sometimes the air gets colder."

"Because that's not cliché of a ghost."

Rosella had to agree with Pugsley. "True, but I didn't make up the fauxlore. Other signs are that the candles goes out. Sometimes it's unintelligible whispering. Those who have claimed to see him say that he is a darker black

74

than the middle of the night and is about the height of an average man."

"So someone wearing all black…"

"Could be trying to pass for the lore's version of the Midnight Man." Rosella had to smile at the idea that maybe their elusive killer who had delusions of being a ghost wasn't as elusive as they thought he might be. "Humor me—how is he even getting into these places, again?"

"In three of our scenes, we found open windows. Others had some entries unlocked. One, we suspect the UnSub might have had the garage code. No signs of forced entry. Whoever did this, they covered their tracks well."

Heading back in, she saw a boy who couldn't have been on the force for very long stand sheepishly at her door, as if he was being called into the principal's office.

"I don't bite. Come have a seat."

Agent Wednesday came in and handed her a copy of Prynne's report. Scanning it quickly, she looked up at the officer. "You might have potentially seen the UnSub Friday night."

"I tried to catch him, I even called it in. But he ditched me in the woods and I just moved here not that long ago and he moved like he grew up around here—"

Rosella nodded, cutting him off. "Can you give me a physical description?"

"I couldn't see his face or hair or anything. He had it all covered in a ski mask. I imagine he was hot under there."

"But height, build?"

75

"Umm, around six foot, athletic build. Whoever had to be in great shape to cover terrain like that as fast as they were."

"Did you hear him say anything?"

"No, but there was this recording. I'd gotten lost in the woods and all of a sudden it sounded like something they might play in a horror movie. I couldn't make anything out but there was whispering everywhere. It gave me the creeps."

"You said *him*, earlier."

"I'm fairly certain you're looking for a guy."

Rosella had assumed as much as well but it was nice to get some confirmation from the one person who might have laid eyes on her UnSub. "Thank you for your time, Officer Prynne."

"Of course, ma'am." He got up and quickly made his way out of the room. Rosella turned to her wall of suspects and took down all the female pictures, keeping them handy in case new information came to light. While that eliminated less than half of her suspects, she would take what she could get right now.

For late September, and especially for Long Island, the weather was amazing. Rosella couldn't help but put her windows down to enjoy the day as she drove back to her hotel. A nearby contact had been rather helpful about a piece of information but she wanted to confirm her suspicions with Dr. Crowdell before she got her hopes up.

Avoiding the interstate and hoping to clear her head, Rosella drove down a backroad but slowed down as the smell of bar-be-que caught her attention. To say nothing of the large cloud of smoke billowing from the woods.

What part of a burn ban did people not quite understand?

Who was having a bar-be-que out here?

Slightly ahead, she noticed a couple of police cars and pulled in behind them. Officer Gina Farnworth got out of one of the cars and Rosella waved. "What's cooking?"

"Forest fire, third one this week."

"You don't smell it?" Rosella took a couple of steps towards the woods, trying to pinpoint just what was burning. "How far away?"

"Bout a quarter mile. I just got here myself."

"Well, lead on."

Rosella fell in step with the officer and the two began their trek. The smell grew stronger, as did the smoke that clinging to the area.

"This one got a little out of control. Forest is dry, we need some rain pretty desperately around here. Luckily, none of the houses nearby were damaged and it's mostly out."

"Have there been a lot of these lately? I know you were called out to one the other night."

"The last few weeks there have been some here and there."

The pair arrived at a taped off area where a CSI team was investigating what looked to be the remains of a campfire. An officer nodded to them as they ducked under the tape and Rosella took in the scene.

The smell of bar-be-que was really strong here but it didn't quite make sense.

"What happened here?"

"There's a home just through those woods and the owners called it in. Seems like it started here and made its way to towards the highway. Luckily the fire department was able to stop it before it made it that far."

"Does someone have a pair of gloves?" Rosella knelt down, looking at the fire. She saw a pair being handed to her out of the corner of her eye and took them, sliding them on before turning over one of the stones in the circle.

"You know, the appendix is one of the mysteries of the human body. Science hasn't quite figured it out yet. There's the assumption that it has something to do with the immune system, but most people consider it to be a generally useless organ."

She looked up to see everyone staring at her, odd expressions on all their faces, and she smiled at their confusion. "Can someone get me an evidence bag? Also, we're going to need to bag up all of this ash."

"Why?" Officer Farnworth brought her the aforementioned bag.

Rosella picked up an appendix from where it had fallen in between stones. Where it had apparently been protected from the flames. Holding it up in her hands, she smiled. "Because the useless organ finally has a use."

It had taken some digging, but she had some ideas about the murder weapon and with a nod to the receptionist made her way back to Dr. Crowdell's office. It was already several days after the second set of murders and she felt bad that she hadn't made it back here yet.

Before she could make it all the way back to his office, Dr. Crowdell came out and met her part way.

"I have to say, it's not every day I get to work alongside a forensic anthropologist."

"A lot of us tend to find a home base and only work cases in that area. I'm one of the few willing to travel, and even I have my specialty."

"Forensic Mythology."

"That's right." She pulled back the sheet on one of the second round's victims, Winona Begum, and ran a hand alongside it. "He was more comfortable this time around. Like he practiced."

"What do you mean?"

"He might have been satisfied with the first group. That is, until he got the media's attention. I think our UnSub has a bit of an ego. The second round is more clean, more defined, more show-offish."

"Any leads on the murder weapon?"

Rosella sat her bag on the counter away from the bodies and pulled out a bundle, unwrapping it to reveal several knives. "I asked around to my contacts, and compared the myth being used to the idea that they are using a knife. Most of them tended to agree that an athame is being used."

"A what?"

"An athame. A knife used in witchcraft, mainly wicca, for various rituals." Rosella picked one up. "Our killer is trying to mimic a myth so he'd use a supposed magical blade in

79

his killings. Fauxlore hodgepodge—he needed a knife, so he picked something appropriately magical from another thread of myth and religion. My sources tell me that these are our best bet. Different shapes to the blade which would account for you thinking there's a second knife involved. Athames don't have a required form—it's a ceremonial rather than 'taxinomical' definition—so he's free to be creative.

"But look at this wound..." She brought a magnification tool over the wound. "Look at how smooth this wound is compared to Sam Watts'." Bringing it over to the other body, she showed Dr. Crowdell her point. "Our guy is much more confident. Tell me, doctor, did he change up the chemical compound?"

"It's more refined, yes."

"He studied what he believes he did wrong and perfected it."

"What does that mean?"

"It means I was right." Rosella took off the rubber gloves and threw them in the right container. "He's not done. He wants to claim his place with the Zodiac and, God help us, Jack the Ripper. He wants people to remember the Friday Fiend."

By Wednesday, Rosella was officially frustrated. Every lead she and the FBI seemed to chase ended in a dead end. There were too many assumptions they had to make, too many leaps to come to a conclusion. Even if they caught the right man based on that, it wouldn't matter because a good lawyer would get him off on unsubstantial evidence.

Plus, she needed a name for her agency. Something fun and catchy that would stand out, yet not make her look unprofessional. Not like Psych out of Santa Barbara, because she wasn't entirely convinced that that wasn't them just saying *Gotcha*.

This case could help her launch her agency. She knew that. It wasn't why she was doing it, but she knew at the end of the day that the FBI was seeing if she was someone they could use. She desperately wanted to be able to help more people and an FBI contract would go a long ways towards it.

Then there was this case. It didn't always make sense and made Rosella glad she spent all of her high school years in a book. That, and made her glad she up and skipped one of them. But this myth, one that she still didn't see the point of, deserved to live on the creepypasta wikia and sites like that. Ten innocent kids didn't deserve to have it brought to life at their expense.

Plus, she was on her second punch card for Sense and Sensibiliteas. She was starting to wonder if she had a problem.

Rosella peeked outside and saw the horde of reporters that seemed to camp outside the police station. Rosella had taken to sneaking in the back entrance of the station to avoid them. One could only take but so many questions about her credentials, her potential move, her inability to solve this case, and insinuations—such as that

Temperance Brennan would have solved it already.

Her phone rang and it broke her thoughts. Looking down, she saw it was her little sister. "What's up, Hannah?"

"How far are you from the city?"

"I'm in *a* city right now."

"Don't get sarcastic with me, Rosie. You know what I mean."

Rosella laughed. "I'm about ninety minutes from the Big Apple."

She heard a sigh. "I'm so jealous."

"I'm working, it's not like I have time to take in a show or anything."

"But you're close to *the* city. With you and Matthew leaving, Mama and Papa are never going to let me out of the house."

"You're sixteen. You've got a couple of years before you should be thinking of leaving the house, regardless."

"You left at sixteen."

"I graduated high school at sixteen." Rosella rolled her eyes. "Let's talk when you have your PhD."

"Please, I'm not sure I can handle that much school."

"How are Mama and Papa?"

"The usual when you're off on a case. Rosie did this, Rosie did that, did you see Rosie on TV? Don't get me wrong, I am instantly the cool kid at school when one of your cases gets *national attention* because everyone wants to know about Forensic Mythology."

"You could study it too." Rosella couldn't help but teasing her sister.

"*We'll see*. Did you find a place in DC yet? I want to come visit you and use it as an excuse to get out of here."

"See? I'm good for something. But no, I haven't. And we both know you hide at my place enough."

There was a sigh on the other end. "I should just sneak away and come visit you."

"First, I'm working. Second, Mama would kill you and then me."

Hannah laughed. "But we could have an adventure in the Big City. I could sneak on a plane, surprise you at work. It'd be so easy! You wake up, and there's your *favorite* sister, ready to see a show!"

"I only have *one* sister. And *not* when I'm working a case where he's targeting people your age."

"Hannah!" Rosella's mom's voice rang out from somewhere on Hannah's age. "Come help me with dinner."

"I'LL BE THERE IN A SECOND, MAMA."

Rosella had to rip the phone away from her ear as Hannah yelled into the phone as well. "Sorry, Rosie."

"It's okay, I didn't need that ear, anyway. I'll text you later. Bye, Hannah."

"Bye, Rosie."

Rosella hung up and turned up her music as she stared at the Victim Board. She needed to make some sort of progress because in just over forty-eight hours the UnSub could strike again.

And she felt no closer to him then when she got here. She would have thought by this point that she would at least have some answer. And maybe she did. But still, she had far too many questions.

Those unanswered questions could get more kids killed.

Why had she set her alarm for this early? Turning off the alarm, she wanted to hide back under the covers when she saw that it was Friday and she had just under eighteen hours to discover the UnSub's identity, or more kids would be at risk.

Forcing herself out of bed, she set the coffee pot to brew hot water for tea. It was ready for her when she came out of the bathroom. Pouring a cup, she let it steep, while she booted up her laptop. Nothing had happened during the night.

Huntington's paper was covered in articles talking about the case, her, the FBI, the school, the previous five victims, The Nest, anything and everything they could write about to not only fill pages but feed the hungry extended audience this crime spree had provided them with.

But Rosella couldn't help but wonder which five kids wouldn't live to see the sun tomorrow. And what was with the number five? Agents Pugsley and Wednesday thought that that was all he could do in about three and a half hours and while part of Rosella was inclined to agree with them, in the spirt of being thorough she had to wonder if that had some significance to her

UnSub. There had to be a clue there. If one really wanted to mix lores, the number seven or thirteen would have been a better fit. So why five?

There was the potential that he was going to escalate. But to what? He was on point with the lore last week, so what could he do to top himself?

Taking a sip of her tea, Rosella peeked out the window to see the sun coming up and with a groan realized that there were reporters already outside the hotel. Waiting for her. Couldn't they wait to annoy her until it was a more decent hour? But the closer they got to Friday, the more vicious they'd become.

Shutting the blinds, she pulled out her information on the Midnight Man as well as the reports from Dr. Crowdell. It had become her daily routine to go over the various files regarding this case before she made her way to the station. She might stop by the school on her way and check to see if Charity and Michael would be coming tonight. Though she wouldn't be surprised if they did; they'd frequent the station in case she or the FBI had any questions regarding The Nest.

That and she had a feeling that a lot of the students wished there was something they could do to help catch their classmates' killer.

The TV did nothing to distract her as all the new stations were talking about it. Even *Good Morning America* was going on and on about this. The eye of the nation, and perhaps the world, were on her. She knew how Frederick Abberline felt.

And she knew that that was what her UnSub wanted. He wanted the fame.

He wouldn't stop until they caught him.

Until then, he might get more and more unpredictable.

She needed something comfortable to wear and turned to see some of the things she'd picked up at the local mall. When she'd packed, she hadn't planned on being gone from her apartment for almost a month. At least, that was her justification to go shopping.

She quickly got dressed and loaded the files into her bag. Satisfied that no disturbing crime scene photos were left out for housekeeping to find, she made her way to the lobby to grab breakfast.

It was going to be a long day.

She had just over two hours before the game might resume for the third week in a row and it looked like a storm was brewing.

Perfect.

Just perfect.

The parking lot of Sense and Sensabiliteas was almost empty as she pulled in to get one last tea before setting up camp at the station.

As she opened the door and a bell jingled and she stepped into the familiar cafe.

"Dr. Tassoni! The usual?" Orlando Toffler called from behind the counter.

"Is it a sign that I've been here too much that you know it offhand?"

"Possibly." He started shuffling around the counter.

"You're in here early."

"It's a bye-week, I offered to close up the shop and get an early start on paperwork." He moved behind the counter preparing her drink. He looked outside. "Storm's brewing. Not a good night for a game."

She looked out the window as the clouds seemed to thicken before her eyes. "Hopefully one isn't played."

As the rain poured down and the thunder boomed, Rosella almost wanted to laugh at the cliché weather.

It had been two weeks since the first murders and there were ten families who wanted answers she didn't have. And the clock told her that she was within a half hour of people potentially playing this stupid game again.

"Why would they still play?" Michael yelled from his usual spot in the break room.

"Because your generation is inherently media obsessed and stupid." Rosella poured herself another cup of tea, taking in the corner the two had taken over.

"Thanks." Charity glanced up from where she was typing.

"Anytime." Rosella took her tea into her "office" and lit a few candles trying to relax herself. What would wave three bring?

What made the difference between the two weeks? Granted, she still thought it had something to do with the media attention he was getting. #FridayFiend had been trending on Twitter for over a week now. She really hated that nickname. Couldn't they have at least done #MidnightMan or #MidnightGame or something?

It was a question that had plagued her since the victims had shown up. Why care in round two?

And what would round three bring?

The power flickered for the third time that night and she wondered if more than the players would be left in darkness tonight.

Her computer chimed, letting her know that it was midnight.

The game had begun.

She stared at the wall of victims which was getting larger than her wall of suspects. Who stood to gain from these murders? The more she thought about it, the more she thought that the key lay in the first five victims.

> Victim 1 - Ashley Coats
> Victim 2 - Edwin Finnegan
> Victim 3 - Shay Hanley
> Victim 4 - Sam Watts
> Victim 5 - Brooke Passingham

So, why these five victims? Rosella stared at the list, the one she'd had for over a week, the faces and lives she'd memorized. But in her gut she knew that these five held the key.

Or better yet, at least one of them. Rosella stared at the first five faces. What could someone stand from the death of one of these kids?

Nothing worth killing over. Sure, some kids got parts in a play, or a seat on the SGA, a first string spot on the football team. But even knowing what her friends at Quantico said, she couldn't see how any of this would drive anyone to kill. And why would they use the Midnight Man for that matter?

The power flickered again as Rosella was sure the thunder caused her tea glass to rumble. She paused to take a sip, wincing slightly at the now-cold tea. Rosella let out a groan in frustration. Even after being in this town for over a week, she still had more questions than she had answers. People didn't get it doesn't work like on TV.

But Rosella realized that she herself had lofty goals and wanted to solve this, to get it over, to prevent the kids who were playing in this awful weather from having to deal with what might be facing them.

"Dr. Tassoni?" Officer Farnworth stepped in. "Gina?"

"The FBI agents want you."

Rosella nodded and made her way to their conference room carrying a candle with her just in case. Inside, she saw a frustrated pair of agents. "You two look as happy as I feel right now."

Pugsley eyed her candle. "Jumping the gun a bit?"

"I lit them to relax me, keep me thinking, and to help me forget that my alarm went off before seven this morning. Why is it that crime happens at an odd hour of the night? Three in the afternoon is a very nice time of day. But no, we must respect the lore and keep us up to midnight, or, worse, the true witching hour."

Both agents nodded in agreement.

But Rosella wasn't done. "But no, they go on creepypasta sites, and NoSleep, and all of these sites. They see this Midnight Man and decide that that's who they want to imitate." Letting out a sigh, Rosella plopped into one of the chairs. "You summoned me?"

"Do you think he will strike in the storm?"

"I'm thinking he still will. After all, this weather is going to hinder the officers out on patrol. If Officer Prynne is correct, our UnSub is going to have no trouble maneuvering through this weather."

The lights flickered again. "And the town might be dark if this keeps up. Who knows, he could expand his demographics."

"But to stay true to the lore, he can only attack the people who summoned the Midnight Man."

"He didn't overly care in round one, so I wouldn't be surprised if he deviates again, in new ways." Rosella looked outside at the storm before glancing at her phone. The game had started and they had no idea who their next victims were. The group had lost a little steam with the second round of murders but there was a still about a one in ten chance that any member of that group wouldn't live through the night.

And she didn't like the odds that high.

Nodding to Pugsley and Wednesday, she made her way into the bullpen and watched as the third shift tried to keep the city going while facing impending murders. This UnSub wanted attention, now he had it. On top of the local police and sheriff's departments, the state police were patrolling the city and the FBI had a couple of teams coordinating with the agents inside the station.

Taking a few deep breaths, she made her way back into her makeshift office and put the music back on. At this point she was mostly just on call in case there was a sighing or a body was found early. But she couldn't help but feeling helpless.

And she didn't like to feel helpless.

With one final flicker, the power went out in the station and the candles she had put on the table casted an eerie glow on the room. Flashlights shone in the bullpen and Rosella grabbed a candle and made her way out, laughing at the irony that she was now mirroring the movements of the game players.

Rosella wandered the pitch black station, candle in hand. Reports said that over half the town was without power and she couldn't help but wonder if the players had even noticed yet.

Outside, the storm continued, and Rosella found herself hoping she could remember the path to the evidence room. She was tired of feeling useless and hoped that looking over everything that had been found for the case.

Her footsteps echoed on the stairs. It reminded her of why people were afraid of the dark.

Why was she skittish? She wasn't afraid of the dark—hadn't been since she was little. In fact, last she checked, she made it a habit to go into the dark and chase the scary things lurking there.

Why would anyone want to play this game three weekends in a row?

Quite frankly, why would anyone want to play this game at all?

It felt like she was thinking in circle after circle and she needed something, anything, to break the cycle.

Rosella had been surprised when they'd shown her the evidence room. It was a large for Huntington, about the size of a high school gym.

Metal racks made it into a giant maze. Dead ends were common. It was clear they'd added racks as necessary, but not in the most organized way.

She hoped she could find her way to the "Friday Fiend" evidence.

At least there were no windows, down here, for the lightning to cast it's eerie glare.

Just the thunder and her candle, now.

And her echoing footsteps.

Muttering the case number under her breath, Rosella held her candle to the cardboard boxes. Not for the first time she wondered what she hoped to gain from this little excursion.

Another set of footsteps echoed through the room. She stopped.

Maybe she wasn't the only one who had the same idea.

"Hello?"

Perhaps announcing her presence was a good idea, since most of the people remaining in the station were armed.

No one answered her, yet the footsteps come closer still.

Rosella took a few deep breaths and reminded herself that it was illogical to be afraid of the dark.

Best case?

It was someone with headphones on and they hadn't heard her.

Worst case?

She really didn't want to think about it.

What had she said about chasing the things lurking in the dark?

"Hello?" Even though she felt like the was talking to herself, talking made her feel better as the footsteps creeped closer.

Then again, with the acoustics, she couldn't be sure.

Giggling caused her to look away. Footsteps raced a few aisles over.

The giggling sounded familiar, though she couldn't quite place it.

She stopped in her search of the evidence for the case and followed the sound of the giggling. The flicker of candlelight caught her attention.

"Hello?" Rosella followed the candlelight. "Is someone here?"

The other candlelight seemed to pause and Rosella power walked to the aisle and stopped cold.

"Hannah?"

Her little sister waved at her, wearing one of Rosella's sweatshirts. One she had caught her stealing dozens of times.

In her hand, Hannah held a candle and there was a grin on her face.

"Hannah, what are you doing here? You can't be here. You shouldn't be here."

Hannah skipped down the aisle and circled around. But when Rosella tried to find her she was nowhere to be found.

And she'd gotten turned around and still needed to find the evidence from this case.

"Here we go." Turning to the shelf that finally displayed the right number she looked at what evidence there was. Was there something here that could help her put all these pieces together. And there was part of her wondering why she had decided she needed to do this at two in the morning in a station without power.

The second set of footsteps stopped and Rosella looked up from the ten pieces of blood-stained paper with ten names she knew oh so well. A black figure stood between her and the exit.

She hated clichés.

He seemed content to watch her and she was content to study him.

It was a him. Suspicions were correct on that. He looked to be around six feet tall; she'd guess around 225 pounds and certainly an adolescent.

Whoever was imitating the Midnight Man was probably a student at the school.

What could push someone so young to do something like this?

"I'm assuming I'm addressing the Midnight Man?"

Rosella eyed the figure. It was dressed so fully in black she could hardly see him.

The lore said that the Midnight Man was blacker than the night in which he haunted...

Rosella forced herself to focus on the Midnight Man. It was a person, someone who had decided to end the lives of ten of his classmates.

"Why?"

The question was out of her mouth before she could think it through.

She hadn't expected an answer so she wasn't surprised when silence met her once again.

Movement caught her eye and she watched the figure pull out a knife. She'd been right about it being an athame. The silver knife shone in the flickering light of her candle.

She wasn't completely sure he was there.

It didn't quite make sense.

Taking a second to calm her breathing, listing various bones (this time the ones of the arms) usually did the trick, Rosella evaluated her options.

"Clavicle, scapula, humerus, radius, ulna."

Her phone was upstairs. Why had she left her phone upstairs?

Why was she down here in the first place?

She took a step away from the killer, her eyes unable to leave the knife.

"Scaphoid, lunate, triquetrum, pisiform, trapezium, trapezoid, capitate, hamate."

The killer stood between her and the door. *Of course he did.* She backed away.

"Metacarpals, phalanges... I'm running out of arm bones here..."

This meant he was here and not out killing who knew how many kids. Since the power had gone out shortly after the game was supposed to begin, there was a chance that no victims were taken.

"Femur, patella, tibia, fibula." Bones of the leg, it couldn't hurt, right? She really needed to find a new calming mechanism.

Why had she come down here without her phone?

"Tarsals, meta—"

The figure took a step closer to her and Rosella looked around hoping that something on these shelves could help her escape.

She didn't want to retreat back, further into the room further from the exit—

But he blocked her only path out.

Evidence or not, something here had to be able to help her.

Help her do what?

"Just what is the Midnight Man?"

Rosella turned to see Hannah wearing an eager expression. "Hannah, get out of here."

"You didn't answer my question, Rosie."

"I quite frankly think this whole game is made up nonsense some insane fan of *that show* devised. There's some elements to it that lend credibility to my theory. Salt, for example, wasn't known for protective barriers until the *Supernatural* 'writers' decided thus."

She made her way to the back wall, the Midnight Man following her with a steady, heavy pace. Hannah moved with her and Rosella tried to keep her little sister as far from the killer as she could.

She took a chance, scurrying along the wall to duck down another aisle, listening for the sound of footsteps as she quietly made her way towards the door.

"Most ghost hunters you talk to will laugh at the idea of salt repelling a ghost. Quite frankly, most will tell you that the spirits deserve more respect than flinging salt at them."

No more footsteps yet.

Had he moved since she went down this aisle?

"We both know better. That the person hiding behind that ski massk is just that, a pershon." She felt herself slurring, shook her head.

Rosella peered through a gap in the shelves. For some reason, the figure hadn't moved except to turn and face her direction. The athame was still in his hand.

Why hadn't he moved?

Should she have stayed with the evidence?

What if he'd come to destroy it?

Did he care about her at all?

Was her life worth that evidence?

"Hannah, I don't know what you're doing here and quite frankly I'm not looking forward to the lecture I'll receive from Mama tomorrow when she discovers you snuck out and flew to New York. But you need to get out of here. I can't...I can't have you in here."

Turning around, Hannah was nowhere to be found.

She circled, peeking out at the aisle she'd originally come from.

He stood still.

He faced her.

He extended his knife toward her.

She took a step backwards, not wanting to put her back to the figure. Her legs felt heavy. Every step was a mile long.

Footsteps reverberated, deafening, as the Midnight Man approached.

Rosella took a few steps back, trying to ignore the fact that his stride was longer than hers. It didn't help that the only light in the room came from the solitary candle she held.

Where was the door?

It was close, wasn't it?

It was on this side of the room, right?

Why was she down here again?

Hannah had gotten out, right? What was she even doing here. She shouldn't be here. She told her no.

Her mother was going to kill her when she found out.

An odd smell caught her attention and she looked to see what it was. A broken box. Inside, rows of glass jars preserving evidence in alcohol.

She shouldn't have looked.

Hannah came charging down the aisle beside her. "Rosie, isn't this game fun? I'm working the case with you."

"I told you to get out of here." Rosella looked around, trying to find the Midnight Man. He was nowhere to be seen. "Get out of here. He's here."

Was she still slurring? Hannah didn't understand.

"What killer? It's a silly little internet game." Hannah smiled at her before passing her by to head down the aisle. "And I'm winning."

"You win until you don't. Just get out of here." She tried to grab her, but her hand didn't work.

The figure reappeared beside Hannah and to Rosella's horror, Hannah paused beside him.

"Hannah! Get away from him!"

Her candle went out and Rosella took off as Hannah was plunged into darkness.

Three seconds. Hannah had three seconds to relight her candle cording to the lore. Rosella ran towards where she had last seen her.

A scream broke the silence.

Holding her candle out, she found Hannah already on the ground, lying in a pool of her own blood.

The organs were already missing. She tried not to look at the gaping wound. Or the blood seeping into Hannah's *Wicked* sweatshirt. Or her eyes…

"Hannah! No…no…you can't. This…"

The figure was right beside her, athame raised to strike her. She dodged out of the way, slamming into the shelf. Pain shot down her shoulder as it collided with the edge and a few feet away, she heard the sound of breaking glass.

The athame came at her again. It slashed down her right arm as her candle crashed to the ground.

Rosella flung her foot up. She slammed into the figure.

He stumbled, just as the candle rolled into the shattered glass.

The candle licked the alcohol eagerly and sizzled its way across the puddle, towards the row of cardboard boxes on the floor.

Where is the nearest fire extinguisher?

Lazily, she looked down at her arm.

It was covered in blood.

To her surprise, it didn't really hurt.

It was a lot of blood, not to hurt, and she almost laughed.

The fire reached the shelves and began eating away at the cases.

Burning plastic filled the air.

She'd lost sight of the figure.

Where was the exit?

Why didn't her arm hurt?

It should be a blinding pain.

The gash was deep.

Why didn't it hurt?

Was it too funny to hurt?

The crackling was steadily growing.

She yelled over it. "If you hadn't disabled everything, we'd have sprinklers. A fire alarm!"

The smoke made her eyes tear up and she coughed, getting another whiff of alcohol.

The fire glowed.

Did it give her enough to find the door?

She should move.

She took off, stumbling, running to the end of the aisle. If memory served, she should come out relatively near the door.

She hoped.

Coughing again, she tried to listen for the second set of footsteps but the fire was too loud. It consumed every other sound.

Her arm was going from slight stinging to throbbing pain making it harder and harder to ignore.

That made sense.

Lightheaded.

Was it from the blood loss or the smoke?

Heat pounded against her back as she made it to the end of the aisle.

Where was the door?

And where was he?

It was nearby, she hadn't gotten that turned around. At least, she didn't think she had.

She settled on a direction and ran. Vibrations, thudding along the concrete behind her, caught her attention and she turned to see the figure coming out of an aisle right behind her.

And Hannah, she'd lost sight of her body. Why had Hannah been there, who had let her downstairs, why hadn't Rosella been able to save her? Rosella sunk to her knees.

Rosella couldn't hold back the scream of pain as the black figure grabbed her bad arm and yanked her up, the pain intensifying in a way that Rosella didn't believe possible.

He yanked her again.

She screamed in pain.

The knife was by her face.

She tried to punch him, and watched her fist go out as though it belonged to someone else.

She caught him across the face. With a right hook that swung like a club.

He staggered, and tumbled, taken off-guard.

He was solid.

A person.

Not a ghost.

Rosella backed up, the figure matching her step for step. She turned to see

BOOM.

A fresh wave of heat pounded against her.

It flung her backward. Towards the door. She almost missed the sight of the athame flying past her. She grabbed the door. The Midnight Man staggered to his feet.

She used the knob to stay upright and slid the bolt shut.

But Hannah was in there…

She took a few deep breaths, in and out, in and out coughs breaking up the breaths as she went. The hallway was pitch black but she stumbled along it, reeling along the wall, scraping her bloody arm as she groped for the stairs.

She needed to get out.

She had to get out.

102

BOOM.

Behind her.

She hoped to any deity who wanted to listen that the gas line didn't run underneath that room.

The sound of footsteps made her freeze.

Had he gotten out?

How had he gotten out?

It took a second but she realized that it was the sound of someone coming *down* stairs and she followed it.

She collapsed on the landing. Someone with a flashlight stood above her.

She coughed Hannah's name, and dropped to her knees.

It all went black.

The Dynamap was the first thing Rosella heard. Keeping her eyes closed and her breathing steady, she checked her surroundings.

The Dynamap meant she was in a hospital. The sterile smell confirmed it.

Biting back a groan, Rosella opened her eyes and found herself in a good sized hospital room. There were some balloons, a few flower arrangements, a stuffed bear wearing Huntington Prep's colors with the logo on the shirt, and to her surprise, Hannah slept on the couch.

Wait.

"Hannah?"

The Dynamap let out a loud beep. Hannah stirred. Rosella looked down at her arm and saw it was pretty heavily bandaged, and splinted if she felt it right. It was also braced against her chest so that her shoulder was immobilized.

Though she was surprised she could feel that much considering the amount of painkillers she guessed were coursing through her system right now. Her other arm was covered in gauze and she could smell some sort of cream on it. She could do without the smell of that.

Rosella really wasn't complaining about that. Hannah was here. *She'd known what she'd seen in that room.*

But it was real.

Hannah was here?

"Rosie?"

She turned to see Hannah looking her way and she smiled. "Hey, Hannah Banana." Her voice was wrong. Thick.

"I told you to stop calling me that. I'm not six." Hannah tried to look cross but that didn't last long before she flung herself onto Rosella's bed. "Don't scare me like that."

"How long was I out?"

"Only about fourteen hours. They said you had to get like 100 stitches down your arm and you lost a lot of blood."

"Where's Mama and Papa?"

Oh, this was not good.

She shifted a bit to give Hannah a bit more room which her sister quickly took advantage of settling in beside her. Closing her eyes, Rosella took a deep breath and let out a sigh.

"Went to check us into the hotel. We got here about an hour ago. I felt sorry for the TSA agent who tried to hold us up."

"Did they leave me some water?"

Hannah handed her the cup and she took a couple of sips. "Thanks."

"I should be thanking you. You got Mom to fly me within 90 minutes of New York City."

"Good to know I'm good for something." Autopilot, more than anything else.

The door to her room opened and Sheriff Peake walked in, smiling when he saw her awake. "You're looking better than the last time I saw you. You gave us quite a scare, Dr. Tassoni."

"Did everyone get out of the station okay?"

He nodded. "We were already evacuating because of the explosions when you were found in the basement. Everyone got out of the building before the fire hit the gas line."

Rosella bit her lip. "Did you find anyone else down there?"

"Should we have?" Sheriff Peake grabbed a chair and sat down beside her bed. "If you feel up to it, mind telling me what happened?"

Recounting the events of the previous night gave Rosella a chance to process how close she'd come to death. She hesitated when she hit the part about her hallucination, she knew now that that was what that had been. Hannah took her hand as she explained it to Sheriff Peake before finishing her tale.

She turned to Hannah. "You weren't supposed to be there."

"I wasn't there. I'm right here." Hannah laid her head on Rosella's shoulder. "Trust me, I'm going to be here to annoy you for a long, long time."

Turning back to Sheriff Peake. "The UnSub was about six feet tall, just over two hundred pounds, around sixteen-nineteen years of age judging by his stance. A few people on the board meet that description. We're going to need the body to determine his identity with any certainty."

"It's going to take a few days to dig through that rubble. Besides, last I heard, the doctor wanted to keep you a couple of days."

Rosella ignored this. "Let me know the second you find that body. Last I saw him he was in the evidence room."

"Was there a chance he escaped?"

"Unless he got through a locked door, no." Rosella coughed.

"And it was him? Not a copycat, or…"

"He matched Phryne's description. He was carrying the murder weapon. I'm certain the wound on my arm is consistent with other wounds. It was in the hallway outside the room."

"We got it, when the officers went to check the hallway. Thank you for your help with this, Dr. Tassoni. I'll be back later with an update."

"Thank you, Sheriff."

Sherriff Peake went out as a doctor entered the room. She smiled when she saw Rosella awake.

"Dr. Tassoni, it's nice to see you awake. I'm Dr. Claire Foster. How are you feeling?"

"I'm assuming you have me on the good stuff because I'm not feeling a whole lot. My head is pounding though."

"You have a slight concussion so that's perfectly normal. Plus, we found large traces of a drug cocktail in your system."

"Drugs? Send it to Dr. Crowdell and get him to cross check it with the samples from the recent murders."

"We already did. You were dosed with enough hallucinogens to recreate the seventies. You've got first degree burns over your arms and on your face. That should be fine within a week. But your arm, well you did quite a number on it. Along with the laceration that required over one hundred stitches, you tore the GGL and the CCL ligaments. Our orthopedic surgeon was able to go in and repair the tears."

"But I'm going to be in a sling for awhile?"

"With the severity of the tears, it's going to be a month to six weeks before you can visit the idea of removing the sling and beginning physical therapy."

"Great." Her voice sounded so flat, and distant.

"We want to make sure the drug is completely out of your system and we're going to need to keep an eye on that wound and your shoulder for a few days as well as your burns. I'll be back to check on you in a little while, Dr. Tassoni."

Dr. Foster left and Rosella leaned back into bed with a sigh. "On a scale of one to ten how much is Mama going to kill me?"

"Thirty-two." Hannah gave her a sheepish smile.

"Awesome."

The door to her room opened again and she braced herself as she saw her mother come into the room.

"Rosella Tassoni! Come osi andare in quel seminterrato in quel momento della notte. Potremmo che hai perso. Cosa stavi pensando? Questo non sarebbe successo se non avessi avuto questa idea di antropologia forense bloccato nella tua testa. Se si era appena tornato a casa e ha lavorato nella panetteria come volevamo a voi sarebbe stato male. Avete qualche idea di come ero spaventato quando abbiamo ottenuto la chiamata a un certo ora dispari del mattino dicendo che vi era stato gravemente feriti e sono stati affrettato in ospedale. Potremmo che hai perso, Rosella. Avrei potuto perdere la mia bambina."

Hannah had enough sense to quickly get out of the way before her mother flew to her side. "I'm okay, Mama."

Her father stood in the door way. "Are you really, Pettalo?"

"Today is September 30, 2016. It is 8:34 A.M. Dr. Felix Crowdell performing the autopsy of a John Doe."

"This is Dr. Rosella Tassoni, forensic consultant, assisting with the autopsy. With us is Huntington Sherriff Kristopher Peake witnessing the autopsy. Are you ready to begin?"

The Sherriff nodded his head but remembered the recording. "Yes. John Doe was discovered in the remains of the station around three this morning. Let the record show, that Dr. Tassoni was the last person to see him alive."

"Our John Doe is a male, aged sixteen-seventeen. From the shape of the skull and nasal passage, I can determine that he was Caucasian and approximately six feet, two inches tall weighing around 225 pounds." Rosella was grateful for the recording, having her right hand in a sling and her shoulder braced would make it basically impossible to write for the next few weeks. She'd manage somehow…

"Most of the burns appear to have happened post-mortem. Dr. Tassoni, care to confirm my hypothesis?"

Rosella studied the body, wishing the sling didn't limit her range of motion. There were few smells she disliked more than the smell of a burned corpse.

"The tissue around the phalanges, metatarsals, tarsals as well as the lower parts of the fibula and tibia and pelvis all appear to have happened antemortem. The second explosion, which consumed Huntington Police Department's evidence room, enveloped the room. This conflagration consumed the rest of the body. My professional opinion is he died some time after the second explosion."

"X-rays performed on the body confirm that, Dr. Tassoni."

"The body was found about four feet from the door, face down."

Rosella felt a little guilt. She had suspicion as to who lay before them, and it was her fault that he hadn't be able to get out of there. But at the same time, he was the one who set the trap and trapped himself in the evidence room.

And it had been her or him.

Remains of clothing was stuck to the tissue of the body due to the fire and the mask was going to be hard to remove.

Her job here was almost done. She watched as Dr. Crowdell continued his autopsy, offering opinions and advice here and there as he cut open the body and examined it further. The sling limited her from actively taking part in the process.

She picked up the right arm and saw what looked like scar tissue on the ulna. "Do either of you know anyone with a scar on their right arm? Looks to be several years old. At least five."

Sherriff Peake seemed to think it over. "Five years ago? Rings a faint bell. A dare or something. Sixth grade initiation. The parents wanted to press charges, but…anything to preserve reputation."

Rosella studied the scar some more. "Provided that the victim is seventeen and entered Sixth Grade at age twelve, that could line up. Do you remember the name?"

"Not off the top of my head, but I can get the file sent over." Sherriff Peake left the room to do just that. The autopsy continued, Rosella examining the body while Dr. Crowdell did his usual autopsy. A technician brought the x-rays into the room; Rosella had the technician stay and put them up so she could study them.

She must have hit him harder than she thought, there were some fractures on the bones around the carpals and metacarpals from where he'd tried to catch himself when he'd fallen as well as on the occipital bone, probably from slamming into the shelving unit when the fire started.

Sherriff Peake came back into the room, his face paler than it had been when he left and held out the file for Rosella to see. Easing her glove off, she stepped away from the body and took the file, confirming some suspicions. "Orlando Toffler. We'll of course have to let the dental records confirm it. But I'm confident in declaring that, based on this file and the scar tissue on his right ulna, that we are looking at the body of Orlando Toffler."

"He did all this. Why?"

"You have enough to issue a warrant to search his house and his locker." Rosella studied the file, comparing the scar in the folder to the one on the ulna in front of her. It matched. "I'd also get a warrant to search Sense and Sensibiliteas…that's how it happened?"

"You mean, being drugged drugged?"

Rosella nodded. "If he's the one who did it, it would have had to be in my tea that night. He was the one who made my drink. It would be the easiest thing in the world to dose all his selected targets, too. An extra ingredient in their pre-game teas and coffees."

"Perhaps the answer lies there."

"One football player kills another. And his girlfriend." Dr. Crowdell didn't look up from the body as he joined in the speculation.

"And eight others, don't forget them." Rosella added. "This town won't forget it."

Finding Closure Where They Can
Bridgett Rosso

It was a solemn crowd gathered outside Huntington Prep Thursday for the unveiling of the memorial that took the lives of 10 students a little over a month ago.

But one absence from the event was perhaps the most conspicuous as Dr. Rosella Tassoni could not be bothered to show her face and answer to the parents who no longer have their children because of her inability to solve the case in a timely manner.

This is just the latest string in questionable actions performed by Dr. Rosella Tassoni during the course of her investigation into the crimes by the Friday Fiend.

One wonders what really happened that night when a fire broke out in the Huntington Police Department leaving the evidence room in ashes and the culprit, high school junior Orlando Toffler dead.

Neither Dr. Tassoni nor the Huntington Police Department have commented on the events of that night.

And what is known of Orlando Toffler?

Speculation as to the boy's motive is vast. Due to his untimely demise, the families of his victims might never truly get justice because they may never know what drove him to kill their children.

For that, they have Dr. Tassoni to thank.

They have Dr. Rosella Tassoni to thank for the almost month of scattered classes that will hurt college acceptances and potential athletic scholarships. They have her to thank that their beloved football team has no post-season prospects.

They have her to thank that there was a second round of murders. That's their tax dollars at work that a specialists was called in and it still almost took her two weeks to solve the case and it was at the cost of six lives.

Friends and families of the victims gathered out front of Huntington Prep to pay tribute to the victims of a crime that has changed their community forever. Hopefully, this will help them to begin the healing process.

Alexandria, Virginia
Six Weeks Later

Tossing the newspaper into the trash can outside, Rosella couldn't hold in the sigh at Bridgett's article. She wasn't surprised, more annoyed.

Biting back a hiss, she shifted uncomfortably in the sling that seemed to be plaguing her with no end in sight. Between that and physical therapy she was a long way from putting Huntington behind her.

She smiled up at her new office, then at her window. It gave her a *view* of the United States Capitol. She'd seen better.

She had been lucky to find the building and the rate for the top two floors wasn't bad. It gave her room for a forensics lab, her office, a file room, a place to hold her stash of books, a waiting room, a storage room, and a couple of offices when she managed to hire more staff.

That was on her list to do soon. She could use the help.

"Good morning, Dr. Tassoni." Her secretary, Kiara, looked up as she stepped into the office. "You have some visitors upstairs."

Checking her phone, she reaffirmed that she wasn't late. "Who comes to someone's office before nine—uninvited?"

Kiara gave her a smile and directed her attention to a waiting room a sorts, where a couple of couches and a glass window revealed her guests to be Agents Pugsley and Wednesday.

"Are you serious? Did you at least bring tea?"

Agent Wednesday held up a cup.

"That's why she's my favorite." Rosella took the cup and waved them into the conference room. "What do you have for me this time?"

From the Consultation Files
of
Dr. Rosella Tassoni

The lock gave a satisfying click (satisfying as only the click of the lock to your newly-acquired-office can be) as Rosella entered the office. She turned on the Christmas tree before any of the other lights. She sat her travel mug on the desk, shifting the bag that rested on her good shoulder while trying to balance her phone to her ear.

"No, Mama. I can't take an earlier flight out. I've got things to take care of before I come. I'll be home for Christmas."

Her mom ranted at her, for the fifth time that day alone, about overdoing it.

"Mama, I'll be fine. It's just consulting work. Paperwork and emails. I've got to go. I want to get this done before this storm rolls in."

Hanging up, she hit play on the *Seb's* Christmas album, while waiting as her laptop booted up.

Taking the opportunity, she took a stack of books from her boxes—Bullfinch, McConnell, Gardner, Fisher—a healthy mix of forensics and mythology. She organized them on her shelves until the computer dinged.

Sitting down, she took a sip of her tea before opening her email. While the doctor had said she couldn't do any *field work* for at least another month, he hadn't said anything about *consulting* work.

And wasn't that what the FBI wanted her to do anyways?

She opened the first file...

Locked Room

Marc Sorondo

It wasn't the corpse that troubled him.

In fact, the victim's body, aside from a crimson blossom on the material over her heart, was laid out in a way that was almost decorative. Reclined on the concrete floor, her short skirt was pushed up to reveal just a slice of her pallid thighs. The red lipstick on her mouth contrasted with the paleness of her skin, giving her the look of a sleeping vampire.

It was her surroundings that were troubling. She'd been found in a sub-basement, one without windows or vents to the outside. She'd been found in a room that was completely sealed aside from a single door, a room with a door that opened inward, one which had somehow been closed and bricked up on the inside.

The killer couldn't have escaped. And yet…

Steve leaned back in the desk chair he'd had since college, the old springs in its back creaking as his weight shifted. He slouched down in the chair until he could look straight ahead and see the words he'd typed. They seemed lifeless to him. Whereas writers he so admired, whose books he devoured with the hunger of a starving child, wrote with vitality to their words. They used language in a way that was unique and interesting. That separated them in a fraternity that was so very different from everyone one else.

Steve looked at the words he'd strung together and felt ashamed of them. He'd spent so much time on them and they were without the spark of greatness.

Even though mystery writers usually got less respect than more literary authors, Steve knew that the challenge for the writer of whodunits was two-fold. He must first create a puzzle, a devious and thought provoking yet solvable puzzle. Most people thought they could concoct such a tale; when challenged, holes quickly made the plot unstable. Writing any story is difficult, but it takes a certain type of mind, somehow criminal and scientific and mathematical and artistic, to write a mystery story.

The mystery writer needed the kind of genius required to engineer a mystery and solution that was believable but difficult, a challenge and a reward. But he also needed to write with the skill and artistry of any great writer. In Steve's opinion, the writing of a mystery was the ultimate challenge, one he'd attempted and failed many times.

He had a stack of unpublished stories in his desk drawer. He kept a black folder full of rejection letters from Hitchcock and Ellery Queen and other less prestigious venues on top of the stack of rejected tales. The newest rejection was over a year old.

Steve had become consumed by doubt. He couldn't finish a story, could not bear to do another round of revisions on any of his old pieces. It was all too exhausting…and yet he couldn't let the dream die. Every night, he sat at his computer laboring over words, often erasing as much as he added.

The phone rang, and Steve felt relieved. He grabbed his phone off the desk and got up, turning his back on the computer and his unfinished story. Before he answered, he glanced at the clock; it was just after three o'clock in the morning.

He looked back to his phone. The call was from Jim Carlin, one of the very few guys in the PD who Steve genuinely liked.

"Jim?"

"Sorry to call so late, Steve, but…you need to come down to the Mountain House right away…you know, the divey place on 340?" Jim's voice was ragged, like he'd been talking for hours without a break or even a glass of water to soothe his throat.

"Now? Why?"

"Trust me, Steve. Get dressed and get over here. You're going to want to be involved in this case."

"Be there in five minutes."

Steve walked through the cacophony and the flashes of blue and red flights feeling like he was underwater. Everything felt slow and slightly distorted. He'd been awake since 5:30 the previous morning and it was now pushing 4:00. He'd gone full days without sleep before, but it hardly made him operate at his best.

The Mountain House was an old building, with architecture that gave it the appearance of a family home rather than a restaurant. In spite of his sleep deprivation, he moved towards it with an air of calm authority through the crowds of civilian onlookers and then through bunches of uniformed cops trying to keep those civilians out of the way. He turned his broad shoulders here and there to pass through a narrowing opening without slowing.

It was a zoo.

Jim hadn't said what occurred. Steve began to wonder if something really crazy had happened, something that would cause what seemed to be all the small population of their suburban town to be out rubbernecking at four in the morning. A murder or a rape…they would create this kind of havoc.

Steve walked into the restaurant and nearly bumped into Jim just inside the door.

"Finally." Jim's voice actually sounded worse in person than it had on the phone. "The hell took you so long?"

Jim's uniform was wrinkled in place. Faded patches where sweat had soaked his shirt and then dried formed circles at his armpits.

"You look like crap, Jim."

"Thanks…long day. Come on." Jim headed off and Steve followed. "You're going to lose it."

"What the hell is going on?"

"There's been a murder…but that's not all. The circumstances…Steve. I wouldn't believe it if I hadn't seen it myself."

They made their way up the flight of stairs that ran behind the bar. At the top, they reached a long hall. There was a bathroom visible through an open door at the end of it; two doors led off the hall on either side, one lit by occasional flashes.

Jim led Steve in.

Aimee was there, photographing the body and the scene.

Steve just watched her for a moment, not even looking at the body on the floor. Her movements were fluid. When she held the camera to her eye, it lingered there for an instant before she snapped a picture. She was an artist even when she wasn't trying to be.

The she pulled the camera from her face and let it hang against her chest, held by the black nylon strap that pressed her blonde hair against the back of her neck.

"I figured they'd call you." She smiled as if she were laughing at him.

"Hi, Aim. Why would they call me?"

"Come on, Detective."

Steve just looked at her, knowing her well enough to know that she would go on.

"They had to call you…what do you love more than a good mystery?" She blushed, either out of anger or in embarrassment. Picking up the black bag that housed her other lenses, she headed past Steve and Jim. She walked out the door as she slid the camera from around her neck and over her head.

Steve watched Aimee walk out the door. When he tried to think about their relationship, he always recalled it as a blur of late night conversations, usually over warming beers, about their aspirations, their profound need to create something powerful and wonderful or their desire to bring something into the world that would really last. Those conversations were them at their best. Even now, Steve thought that no one understood him as Aimee did, that no one could. He often thought that was why there hadn't been anyone since her.

Perhaps they had understood each other too well. While they had been a source of support, a critical eye and an encouraging voice to each other early on, they came to repulse each other. They shared constant rejections without any successes. Both saw their failure mirrored in the other; saw their own pain and frustration reflected back at them in every glance.

"You okay?" Jim asked.

"Yeah, sorry. What do we have?" He looked at the body. It was face down, stretched across an area where an ancient hardwood floor met a ratty, tan area rug. The body was laid out, one leg extended straight down and the other turned and bent at an obtuse angle. The arms were out, as if he'd caught himself while falling forward and eased himself to the ground. The face, turned to the left, was visible in profile. The eyes were closed. A single lock of short brown hair contrasted against the paleness of its forehead while the rest of it was smoothed back.

Of the knife, only the wooden handle was visible, pressed up against the victim's back to the side of the spine. It looked to Steve like an old serrated steak knife; based on its placement, he figured it'd been forced between two ribs and into a lung. Blood had pooled around the knife and spilled off the body, cascading over the fabric of the victim's t-shirt to form another pool on the floor.

Steve walked around the body once. It was too neat. Aside from the blood, which had pooled onto a smooth puddle by the body, nothing was disturbed. There was not the slightest ripple in the rug beneath the body, no signs of struggle.

Steve moved around to the center of the room and turned slowing, taking in every detail no matter how minor it seemed. He tried to think of all of it as data, to appreciate everything, just as the Great Detective would have.

The room looked like it had been thrown together piecemeal. None of the furniture matched, and the threadbare rug was spread like a thin layer of dust over a floor that needed more than a few coats of varnish.

To the right was a desk, topped by an old computer, a grey, plastic telephone, and a mess of scattered papers. A spot had been cleared at the front of the desk, a semicircular patch free of clutter. There rested a single bar napkin with something scribbled on it and a clean ashtray, the unadorned back plastic type that restaurants of that caliber used to put out before New York passed laws banning all smoking indoors. In one of the ashtray's notches rested a lone cigarette, unsmoked, while a new box of matches, one with the Mountain House logo printed on it, sat, half-hidden, in the bowl of the ashtray. A trio of filing cabinets stood monolithic and indestructible behind the desk. The two on the ends were a dingy blue-grey, the color of World War II battle ship; the one in the middle was a drab, clerical shade of tan.

To his left was a lounge area. An old couch upholstered with navy blue fabric dotted with small, white anchors sat along the wall. A creaky wood rocking chair, one with a slat missing from its back, sat perpendicular to the couch. Opposite the rocking chair was an old recliner: pea soup green with a wooden handle for the mechanism.

At the center of this area was a low cocktail table that was empty aside from three magazines—a tabloid and two old issues of *Playboy*—and another ashtray, this one made of brown, semitransparent glass and stuffed full of crushed butts of various brands. Some had tan filters while others had white; some were marked by striped rings of corvette red or cotton candy pink lipstick, while others were clean. From this mound of old butts; the room was perfumed faintly with the aroma of stale ash.

On either side of the door were black metal shelves, the kind that belonged in a garage or a workshop rather than an office. These held everything from employees' jackets and Mountain House t-shirts to pint glasses and silverware. Chrome bolts gleamed nakedly where the metal scaffolding was held together. They protruded like misguided teeth, contrasting sharply with the smooth blackness of the shelves.

Steve approached the desk, hoping the scribbled napkin said something interesting. It was written in chicken scratch, bright blue ink against the off-white napkin.

> *2:13—I think Johnny and Chance are trying to mess with me. They didn't want to lose the bet. It's that or*

Steve straightened back up and scanned the room once more, hoping to catch every slight detail. The windows were all closed and locked. There were old burns and spots of ash near the corner of the area rug. Someone had doodled on the cover of one of the *Playboy*s, giving the model a mustache and blacking out her eyes.

"The door was locked?" Steve asked.

"Locked from the inside…also, there were pieces of paper taped around the door to prove it hadn't been opened.

Steven looked bewildered. "Why?"

"There was a bet. The victim, Robert Woodcliff, a regular at the Mountain House, took a bet that he could spend the night here, in the supposedly haunted bar, alone."

Steve nodded. "I see."

"It was the guys who bet against him that actually called us." Jim added.

"How did they know?"

"Said they came back to scare him, but saw him through the window."

Steven nodded again.

"You excited?"

"A guy died." Steve felt guilty, but it was hard not to feel like he'd stepped into on of his own stories...one of the stories he wanted to write but never could. Now, he felt like he was living one.

"Don't screw around."

"The odds of getting a case like this are a million to one. A real mystery...locked room and everything..."

"Now you've got to solve it. You ever come across anything like this in any of your stories?"

Steve thought for a moment. "So far, at least, this is all very Edward Hoch."

"Never heard of him."

"That's because you only read what Oprah tells you to read." Steve gave him a tired smile.

"That was one book. When are you going to stop giving me a hard time about that?"

"Hoch wrote a ton of stories for *Ellery Queen*. He was great at locked room stories. This seems like something he would write; a sealed room, a supposedly haunted bar. Apparently no clues at first glance."

"So what are you going to do?"

"Talk to Johnny and Chance."

John "Johnny" Hemner and Chester "Chance" McGinty sat in separate rooms. Both were in that most awful state of wakefulness: the amount of alcohol in their systems would usually have them drunk as a pair of skunks, giggling and slurring, if not completely passed out. But they were forced into some sort of miserable sobriety by their situation. They sat there, isolated. Their eyes were wide, underlined by dark bags and edged with redness. Johnny sat up, his back flat against the chair, too straight to be comfortable; Chance slouched, his arms crossed over his chest, nibbling at his lower lip.

The shock, the stress induced hormones, were forcing them awake, keeping them alert. Steve knew they would gradually become hungover.

One after the other, Steve sat with them and listened to their stories, occasionally interrupting with a question.

Their stories were basically the same: Johnny, Chance, and Rob had headed to the Mountain House around ten for a few pizzas and quite a few beers. At some point, the topic of the "Mountain House Ghost" came up. Rob had called it a combination of clever marketing and suggestible employees. He had grinned like a little boy who'd just spotted a hidden compartment in a showman's magic trick and said that he knew.

Johnny and Chance hadn't bought it. It was one thing to be unafraid in a bar full of people, all the lights on, beer flowing, and the music blaring from the jukebox. If Rob was so brave, he'd need to be brave in the dark...in the late, empty hours...in the quiet.

They took the issue to Tommy, the Mount House's owner, who had been tending bar. Tommy proposed a wager. He said he'd allow Rob to spend the night in the upstairs office, to prove he wasn't afraid...if he really thought he could last the night.

Last call at the Mountain House was at midnight. The place was empty and locked up by one.

They left Rob in the office. The sealed up the door, so they'd know if he snuck out. Steve asked and both men noted that they had taped paper on three sides of the door, that the space at the floor had not been sealed.

Steve wasn't sure that it would be significant, but he made sure to note it anyway.

From the Mountain House, Johnny and Chance had headed to Bailey's, another bar that was within walking distance, one that didn't close until three. At Bailey's, they drank more and ate Buffalo wings and waffle fries. When the bar was closing, Johnny and Chance decided to go back to the Mountain House to give Rob a bit of a scare.

There was lattice on the outside of the building, one providing a footing for only weeds. Johnny, slight more inebriated than Chance, tried to climb it and fell from halfway up. After laughing for a while, Chance decided to give it a try. He made it to the window. When he looked in, he nearly lost his grip when he saw Rob lying there. He screamed and scuttled down the lattice.

Even drunk as he was, Johnny could tell that Chance wasn't kidding. They called the police, and then stood there in the parking lot, unsure of what to do, waiting.

Steve didn't think the two drunks had killed Rob. The seemed genuinely distraught and their stories lined up.

He looked at the clock and decided to head home and get a few hours of rest. It had been over a day since he'd slept last. Then he'd talk to Tommy, the owner of the bar who'd set things into motion by suggesting the bet.

Steve returned to work after four hours of sleep, a shower, and two cups of coffee. Thomas Dwyer was already at the station, eager to seem cooperative. He sat at a table, sipping a cup of coffee.

"Good morning, Mister Dwyer." Steve walked into the room and closed the door. "I'm Detective Vecchiata. I just wanted to ask you a few questions to try and clear up some of the grey areas in our knowledge of what occurred last night."

"Yeah, yeah, anything I can do to help."

"Now, we were told that this…wager was your idea?"

Tommy nodded, grinning nervously. "Yeah, it was. I didn't think anything like this was going to happen."

Steve sensed that Dwyer would prattle on if there was quiet, that in his nervousness he might let something useful slip. He sat there, his face an unreadable mask, and stared at Dwyer.

"Thing is…the whole haunted thing is good for business. It's basically word of mouth advertising. If there are things I can do to keep people talking about the stupid ghost, I usually do. I figured that, even if Rob stayed the night and didn't see anything, it would still keep people talking."

"By that reasoning…this murder could be good for business."

"What?" Tommy looked around the room as if searching for something. "Listen, a harmless ghost story is one thing…a guy dying…that's not worth an increase in business."

Steve was silent. He just nodded.

"Listen, I don't even believe in that ghost garbage. I've never seen anything weird and I've never tried to make anyone believe it either. People are dumb; they want to believe, so they convince themselves that they saw something or felt something…it's all suggestion. People want to talk about a ghost in the place and it brings in customers…I'd be stupid to squash those rumors."

"So you thought this bet would be harmless?"

Tommy nodded. "I figured he'd pass out on the couch up there and either sleep it off until we opened up or wake up, spook himself over nothing and run out. Either way, it was all supposed to be, you know, a joke."

"That door was locked from the inside…who has a key to it?"

"I do. My manager Kyle has a copy too…that's it."

"And where were you last night between closing and the discovery of the body?"

"Home. Ask my wife. I worked all day yesterday. I got home and was out cold the second my head hit the pillow.

Steve nodded. "Any idea where Kyle was?"

"He's in Aruba on his honeymoon. That's why I've been working so much…why I'm so tired."

Steven nodded again. "Alright, Mister Dwyer. I appreciate your help. If we need any more information, we'll be in touch."

Over the next few days, Steve met with every one of the Mountain House's employees, starting with the ones that had worked the night of the murder. The bar sounded like a monotonous place to work. It seemed like the same regulars were in all the time; they made up most of the place's business. Staff didn't change often…nothing changed often. Even the specials were repeated regularly.

The only break in the status quo was the occasional supernatural encounter. A number of the employees claimed to have seen things move without being touched, to feel an unexplainable cold, to sense a presence when they should have been alone.

Some of the employees mentioned Ana. They said that the ghost had attacked her…that she had quit and never set foot in the Mountain House again.

No one could think of anyone who would want to kill Rob. Nor could they think of anything suspicious.

Steven got to his desk to find a stack of paperwork waiting for him. The Medical Examiner had little to add to the case. The cause of death was exsanguination. Steve had been wrong about the lung; it had been punctured, which would have made his quick death an excruciating one. The time of death was approximately 2:30 AM, which lined up with everyone's stories.

Forensics had dusted the murder weapon for prints and found none. The rest of the room was so full of prints, hairs, fibers, and other evidence that it was all useless. Too many people had spent too much time in the office to pick out any one fingerprint or hair as being that of the killer. The unsmoked cigarette was the brand that the victim smoked.

Steve had nothing to suggest a new direction for the investigation. He ticked off the things that might still be of some importance: the door was sealed, but not along the bottom edge, the cigarette had been untouched, the note suggested that Rob had heard or seen something to make him suspect a prank was being played, and something had interrupted the writing of that note.

Of all the people he'd spoken to so far, none seemed likely to be the killer. Johnny and Chance had been at Bailey's during the murder and had no motive to kill their friend. Tommy had a motive—a stretch, but it was still there—but was at home with his wife. The employees all had alibis and none seemed to dislike Rob very much. A few mentioned that he, like Johnny and Chance, could be a pain if he drank too much, but even then he was only annoying.

Steve decided to go see Ana, to find out what she thought had happened that had scared her so badly.

Ana Watkins lived in a rented apartment over the house of an elderly couple just a few minutes from the Mountain House. The apartment was accessed by an external staircase that ran up the side of the main house.

As Steven ascended the stairs, he wondered what he expected to learn by speaking to Ana. What information of value could she possibly have? He didn't know, but his gut insisted that he talk to her and his mind agreed that it was better to follow every possible lead just in case.

He held his badge as he knocked on the door.

The door opened and a face that was younger than he'd expected peered out. "Yes?"

Steve flashed his badge. "Miss Watkins?"

She nodded.

"I'm Detective Vecchiata. I was just hoping to ask you a few questions."

She looked up at him and he met her gaze. Ana's eyes were hollow. Steve had spoken to quite a few victims of rape. They had a similar emptiness in their eyes, as if being so completely violated had ripped them open and torn out all the living tissue, as if they were a shell of skin and no more.

"What's this about?"

"There's been a murder…at the Mountain House."

For an instant, those hollow eyes were filled with dread. They went wide and the pupils seemed to float in orbs filled with horror and understanding.

"I'm sorry. I haven't worked there in years. I can't help you." She began to close her door.

"Miss Watkins, please tell me what happened to you that night."

She stopped, her face visible through the narrow aperture between the door and the jam. "I filled out a report. You can read it."

"I want to hear it from you, please."

Ana was a small woman, one that would be attractive if it weren't for the look in her eyes and the air of exhaustion about her. She led Steve into a small living room with beige carpet and a light blue couch. She did not offer him coffee.

She sat on a rocking chair and motioned for Steve to sit on the couch. "You won't believe me. I told the police what happened, and they were quick...almost eager...to call me a hysterical woman, to call me crazy."

"Miss Watkins..."

"Ana, please."

"Ana, a man was murdered in the upstairs office at the restaurant. Many of the employees mentioned you and what happened to you up there."

Ana nodded, and Steve fell silent.

"I was counting the night's money, closing everything out so I could head home. I had worked a double so I was really tired. I was at the desk, splitting the money into four piles. At first, I just had a funny feeling…like a chill or like someone watching me."

Ana shivered. She stared off, her gaze rising to the point where the walls met the ceiling.

"I looked around and at first I wasn't sure anything was even there. It was standing in a dark corner, sort of back behind that ratty old couch that they used to keep up there. It sort of blended in, like it was a darker shadow standing in a normal shadow. I couldn't move at first. I just sat there, staring at it, like I was paralyzed. I wanted to be out of there so bad but…my muscles wouldn't move. I was so scared. I couldn't do anything except sit there and be terrified."

She looked at Steve for a second. "Then it came at me."

She looked away and a tear rolled down her cheek. She quickly wiped it away with the palm of her hand.

"I felt like my heart was going to burst. I've never felt fear like that. I was up and running for the door but I felt so slow, so inadequately slow. It scratched my back as I reached the door. I didn't look back though. I ran down the stairs and out the door. I couldn't be in that place."

"A few of the girls and some of the regulars came out and convinced me to come back in, but I wouldn't go upstairs. They called the police."

Ana was quiet for a second. She turned at pulled at the neck of her t-shirt, exposing some of her left shoulder. There were three fat lines of scar tissue running from left to right across the visible portion of her shoulder. They were glossy and pink.

"The cops said that I bumped into one of the metal shelves in the office…that some of the exposed bolts scratched me when I bumped into it…that I got scared and imagined everything else. Next time you look around in there, look at those shelves. The bolts don't match these scratches."

Steve nodded. "I've already seen them…they don't match. Aren't three in a row like that anywhere."

"Well…think what you will then. I don't care if you believe me."

"Thank you for your help. I can see it's difficult for you to talk about it, and I appreciate it."

Ana walked him to the door. She closed it behind him, and he heard the hurried scrabble of fingers over locks and the small, metallic scrape of a deadbolt driven home.

Steve thought about ghosts. He didn't believe in hauntings. He certainly didn't believe that some evil spirit had attacked Ana Watkins or stabbed Rob Woodcliff. He found himself thinking of old *Scooby-Doo* cartoons, of the idea that a fake ghost could be used to hide a real crime. If he pulled the mask from Ana's shadowy attacker, who would he find playing the part of the ghoul?

Steven couldn't be sure of it, not yet at least, but he kept seeing Tom Dwyer's face beneath that mask.

The Mountain House was packed, and Steve couldn't help wondering if the already infamous "ghost murder" hadn't been the reason for the boost to business.

He headed right for the bar. Flashing his badge to the bartender over the shoulders of two guys sitting hunched over pints of beer, Steve asked. "Is Tom Dwyer here?"

"Yeah." The bartender pointed straight up.

Steven nodded and made his way up the stairs and into the hall. Yellow police tape blocked the door to the office. Another door was open on the opposite side of the hall.

Steve approached, walking through a faint cloud of tobacco smoke. He found Tom standing in a room full of boxes. The bar's owner stood at a window, staring out into the darkening sky as he puffed on a cigarette.

"Technically you shouldn't be smoking in here, even upstairs."

Tom turned around at the sound of Steve's voice. "I still think that law's garbage." He took a drag and then flicked the butt out the window. "I should decide if it's okay to smoke in a place I own."

"I actually agree with you on that one. Busy down there tonight."

Tom nodded. "I knew it would be. Like I said, the ghost stuff brings people in. They want to see something crazy."

"Where did the haunting story come from?"

Tom shrugged. "When I bought the place it already had that reputation."

"You wanted that reputation...I recall you saying that you suggested the bet because you wanted to keep the ghost story going."

Dwyer straightened up, stood a little taller, his shoulder back and chest out, like superman in an old cartoon. "What exactly is this about?"

Steve grinned at that. He found that body language telling: Dwyer was subconsciously projecting a righteous anger at the idea of being a suspect.

"Just wanted to clarify exactly how important, financially, the ghost story is to this place, to you."

"Listen, Detective, I understand how it might look, but I've been honest about everything. I didn't kill Rob. I don't know who did. I said I don't believe in ghosts and I don't. I think a person did this...but if people want to come here because of what happened, I'm not going to turn them away. I've got nothing to hide, Detective. Feel free to investigate me all you want."

Steve nodded. He thought it best to leave Dwyer feeling uncomfortable, feeling scrutinized. That feeling might just get under his skin. "Mister Dwyer, we're investigating everyone. Have a nice night."

Steve left. He needed to grab dinner and get some sleep.

After dinner, Steve sat in front of his computer. He could not think of a single word. He stared at the screen, the light making his eyes ache, and realized that he didn't feel the need to write. For the first time in his life, it seemed unimportant.

His love for the genre had developed because he loved the sleuth. He'd been trying to write his own stories because he knew that reality would never offer him the opportunity to be a man like that. He'd never solve the unsolvable like a Hercule Poirot or a Sam Hawthorne; he'd never be as tough or as cool under pressure as a Sam Spade or a Philip Marlowe. Steve had begun making up stories because he couldn't live them.

The thing was...now he could. He was a detective investigating a real locked room mystery. If he could solve it...if he could find the killer and discover the methods by which a crime could be made to seem impossible...he wouldn't need to make a story up.

Steve felt unreal. He felt like a character in someone else's tale, like the creation of some hack writer who had taken far too long to get to the good part of the story.

Steve shut the computer down. He needed sleep. He was overtired and over stimulated and he started to feel like he was going to lose it. He tried to understand his own feelings from a moment earlier, that sense of the unreal that he'd sensed so keenly now seemed crazy.

Steven went to his bedroom. He fell onto the unmade bed; the pillow felt cool and pleasant against his face. He reached down and pulled the sheet up to his waist and thought about Ana Watkins.

He lay in the dark and tried to figure out how a person could seem to be a ghostly figure. As he drifted, somewhere between wakefulness and sleep, he pictured Ana's shadow. In his half dream, the shadowy face was just a mask. He grabbed it. The material was coarse, itchy against the tips of his fingers. Steve pulled the mask away and beneath lay…another shadow.

Steve had hit a wall.

There was no new evidence coming in, no more witnesses or Mountain House employees to talk to…he had every piece to that particular puzzle that he was going to get and there didn't seem to be enough of those pieces to make any sort of picture.

Steve lacked the ever-important data that his favorite sleuth always craved.

He spent a few hours in his office and only succeeded in getting frustrated. His setting, he decided, was stifling his creativity. He needed a fluid mind, one that would flow in unexpected ways and make unorthodox connections, if he hoped to solve the case of the murderous phantom.

He gathered up his files and headed home.

Steve moved the coffee table out of the way so that he had a wide, cleared expanse of carpet at the center of his living room. He stood in the center of this area and began laying out the contents of his files. He worked slowly, placing things in an order that made sense to him. He wanted each bit of data to relate to those near it, to create a web in the hopes that he may recognize some shape to it.

After a while, Steve sat at the center of a ring of information: photos of the body and crime scene, photos of the bar's employees and regulars, written accounts, the Medical Examiner's reports, the old report of the Ana Watkin's incident…it was all fanned out on the carpet, one slightly overlapping the other.

Steve looked at the information surrounding him, taking in the details of a photograph here, reading a passage from his written notes there. Occasionally, Steve though he'd made a different connection, that he'd noticed something previously overlooked, and he'd move a bit of data from one point in the circle to another. He sought patterns. He sought the truth hidden in the details.

He scanned the information and read the notes again and again, moving things when he felt it necessary, reassessing the new connections as his impression of the crime gradually evolved, until he thought he must have it all memorized.

Finally, Steve headed for the kitchen, leaving the ring of information lying on the floor. He'd begun to feel like as much of a failure as a detective as he felt as a writer. In both, he could not make the connections required to reach the climatic scene. His life and art were the same: incomplete.

Steve felt empty. Fate had handed him his dreams and he'd been unable to make anything of them. He again felt that sense of unreality, wondered why the author of his reality refused to show him the image the pieces formed, to let him see through the veil of scary stories and seeming impossibilities to uncover the murderer and his methods.

Then that sense faded. Steve feared that he was cracking under the pressure. He needed to get out, to put the case out of his head for a while.

Steve went to The Porch, a hole-in-the-wall college bar that he'd never matured out of frequenting. As he pulled into the parking lot, he wondered at the number of bars scattered throughout the few small towns that made up the community in which he lived and worked. He wandered what that said about the area, about the people who lived there and kept all those bars in business.

He walked in and found the place nearly empty. There was a quartet of guys in dark t-shirts playing pool on the scratched up, old billiard tables in the back. Another guy, similarly dressed, stood before the jukebox, scrolling through his options.

A guy in a flannel shirt and girl in a pink shirt and tight jeans were playing darts on a Budweiser board that had been hanging in the same place since before Steve had started drinking there.

Two small groups sat at the bar. One group of two couples was preparing to suck down a round of car bombs. The other, three chubby girls drinking bright green martinis, looked longingly at the pool players who weren't drinking enough to be interested.

The man behind the bar was broad shouldered with a big soft belly and a round face. He wore a black polo shirt that stretched tight over his paunch.

Steve sat down at the corner seat nearest the door, far from all of the bar's other patrons. "Hey, Chris."

"How's it going, Steve?" He'd already filled a pint with Smithwick's when he saw Steve enter. He tossed a coaster down on the bar in front of Steve and placed the pint on it. "You investigating that murder over at the Mountain House?"

Steve nodded and took a sip of his beer.

"I bet it was Dwyer. You know he's offering ghost specials and spectral happy hours and garbage like that?"

"You know I can't talk about it."

"I know, I know, I was just saying." Chris looked over his shoulder and saw that two of the three lonely girls had empty martini glasses before them.

"Duty calls." He headed over to them.

Steve though to himself that Dwyer would be the killer in a simple mystery, that he was too obvious to be the killer in a masterfully written story. The killer in a well-written tale would be harder to tie to the murder; he would have a subtler motive.

The door opened with a squeak and Steve felt a gust of outside air blow against his back. He kept looking forward, running through the list of potential suspects yet again.

There was a crowd of voices. Steve recognized Aimee's. His stomach fluttered, felt achingly empty.

That group—Aim along with three other girls and a lone guy—sat over by the dart board, between the double daters and the desperate trio. Aimee was smiling. Steve had always loved her smile. He still did, but he hadn't seen her smile in a long time.

She spotted him. He expected that she would ignore him or that her smile would fade when she saw him. Instead, she smiled at him, said something brief to one of the girls she was with and headed over.

"Hi, Aim."

"I've got big news." She leaned against the bar beside him.

"Good news, it seems."

She nodded. Then, still smiling, she looked into his eyes and they were both quiet for a while. It was a comfortable silence. It felt like old times, good times.

"I sold a photo. It's going to be the cover of a literary journal."

"Really?" Steve smiled now too.

"It's just some no-name journal with a circulation of like four people, and I'll only make like fifteen bucks but…"

"It's just the first…the first of many. Everyone starts small. That's amazing, Aim. That's great news."

Steve waved at Chris. "Do me a favor, Chris. Get Aimee and her friends a round on me."

Chris nodded and set five shot glasses down before Aimee's friends.

"So how does it feel?"

"Fake...I know it's not really a big deal, that hardly anyone will ever see it, but it still feels like a big deal."

"It is a big deal. You got your start. Someday, you'll look back and remember that photo and that journal because it will always be your first."

She nodded. "You're still writing, right?"

"Yeah, as much as I can."

"Good...never give up, Steve. You're good. I've always thought you were good, no matter what happened between us...never give up on that dream no matter how long it takes."

"I won't, Aim. Congratulations."

"Thanks. You want to join us?"

He did.

"No thanks. I'm trying to mull things over...this case. I've got to just think. Thanks though.

She nodded, flashed him another smile, and headed back to her friends.

Steve tried to think about the case, but his thoughts kept going back to Aimee. Then he was overcome by that uncanny feeling again, though this time it was different. He felt fake, but he also felt unimportant, that rather than being the protagonist of his own story, he was a peripheral character in the drama that was the story of Aimee's rise to fame as a photographer. He tried to shake that feeling off; he disliked it, hated it for the way it made him feel. Steve looked at the various people in the bar, at Chris pouring drinks, at the pool players and the double daters, at the dart players and even Aimee's friends and he realized that every one of them thought they were the star. Every one of them thought that they were important, that if not the hero or the heroine, they were at least major characters. Just then, Steve realized that most likely, none of them were.

He felt inconsequential.

Suddenly, he needed to solve this case more than ever. He needed to solve it to establish his importance, his role. He needed to solve it in order to write himself into history, into existence…because if he failed, no one would know of him; if he failed, he would fade away.

Steve walked into the Mountain House and spotted Tom Dwyer behind the bar. Dwyer saw the detective enter and whispered something to the other bartender before heading over.

"Detective, any chance you're just here for a drink?"

"I wish. I need access to the office after hours. I want to look around at night, preferably when it's quiet."

Tom nodded. "I can stay late, let you look around."

"I'd prefer it if I were completely alone, if that's alright."

Tom made a face. "Yeah, I guess that's alright."

Steve went back at 3:30, long after the Mountain House had closed and everyone had left. He used the key Tom Dwyer had given him to get in and locked the door behind him. He didn't bother with the lights downstairs. Instead, he headed right for the staircase behind the bar. He ascended in the dark and then found the switch to illuminate the upstairs hall.

The yellow tape was still stretched across the door to the office at random diagonals. Steve crouched under it and entered. Even with the lights off, by only the moonlight coming in through the windows, he could see where Robert Woodcliff's blood had dried on the floor.

Steve closed the door to the office. Then, for reasons he couldn't quite understand, he locked the door.

The details of the crime and the alleged supernatural activity caused Steve to wonder if there was not some architectural anomaly in the Mountain House. Far-fetched as it seemed, he knew it was possible, in theory at least, that the room had some sort of hidden door, a secret panel or niche, something in which someone could hide or, better yet, a secret passage allowing someone who wanted to seem like a ghost to move while hidden.

Steve walked around the room with the lights out. He already knew that he didn't visually notice anything that suggested a hidden door; he hoped that perhaps he would feel a breeze or a drop in temperature that would alert him of something strange.

After a full circuit of the room he turned the lights on. He flicked the switch and looked around. Rob had likely been sitting at the desk when he'd written his unfinished note. Similarly, Ana Watkins said she'd been sitting there when she sensed something in the dark corner.

Steven went to the filing cabinets behind the desk, to the corner that would be unseen if someone sat to do work or scratch out a note. He inspected it, walls, ceiling, floor, cabinets. He closely scanned every surface, knocked on each one and noted the sound.

He found nothing.

He sat in the chair before the desk. He wondered how many people had sat in that very spot and experienced something they couldn't explain. He looked around the room before leaning back in the chair, which let out a quiet squeak.

Steve realized that he hadn't asked Aimee about the photo that she sold. He didn't know if it was black and white or color, if it was of a person, a flower, a panoramic shot of an incredible view. It could have been anything. He couldn't believe that he hadn't thought to ask her.

Steve noted a chill in the air, as if a window had been thrown open to allow an icy wind to blow over his shoulders. His eyes widened. Some passage had opened; he just new it.

He turned around and drew his gun. He aimed at a dark figure that stood just behind him, where the filing cabinets met the wall.

"Put your hands up. You're under arrest for the murder of Robert Woodcliff and the assault of Ana Watkins."

The figure walked towards the door, towards the industrial looking shelves, and Steve realized that it was no costume. The shadow reached the shelves and picked up a knife.

Steve wondered, if the specter could touch and hold physical objects, could a physical object hurt it? He fired a shot, one that passed through the intangible form and into the wall behind the shelves.

The shadow stood between Steve and the door. A steak knife protruded from the end of one of its indistinct appendages.

All at once it hit Steve and he was profoundly disappointed. A locked room mystery was supposed to involve a trick, an illusion. The writer of such a mystery has entered into an unspoken agreement with his audience: the crime only appears impossible; however, the story will reveal the truth, expose the illusions that made the crime happen and disguised it as an impossibility.

Even as the phantom approached, Steve was not afraid. Instead, he felt cheated, as if the author of all things had broken a rule that even He was supposed to follow.

Steve stood and looked at the specter, at where a face would be on a man, where eyes would be.

There was only darkness there.

He felt outraged. The anger filled him. It had all been a lie. He would no more live out a detective story than he would successfully write one. What had seemed at first a locked room mystery was really a ghost story. That was the only trick, the only illusion.

A ghost story.

That was not Steve's genre. He refused to be a character in that type of tale. He lunged past the specter, heading for the door. He'd run, just like Ana Watkins. He'd run and he'd live and he'd go back to writing.

Steve reached out for the doorknob; then he felt it, between his ribs. Just beneath his shoulder blade, off the left side of his back. At first it just felt like a pressure that had moved into his chest, a warm mass that forced its way inside of him and made it hard to breath. He fell to the floor; face down, his hand still stretched toward the door. It quickly became an icicle, a cold that seemed to start in his heart and gradually spread outward.

For a moment, he fully expected to have his life flash before his eyes. So much of it had been cliché—the failed writer; the bored, small town detective—that the ultimate cliché of reliving it all in the instant before his death seemed a fitting end to the whole mess.

Instead, two thoughts filled his mind as the cold numbed his fingers and toes, then his hands and feet. He thought of all the stories he'd never written and never would. He thought of Aimee, of things he would have done different and things he wished he said.

Regret.

Nothing was more cliché.

Steve's vision became dark. He saw shadows everywhere. He closed his eyes and could no longer feel his body.

Everything but Steve's anger faded. This was not the way things were supposed to turn out...this was the wrong ending.

Steven exhaled for the last time...

To: Agent Audrey Wednesday
From: Dr. Rosella Tassoni
Subject: Mountain House

Seriously, Audrey. I meant it when I said my job is not to tell you whether or not a ghost is real. The first death is interesting, the previous attack on Miss Watkins as well.

Unfortunately, without taking a look at the scene itself, I can't give you specifics on the case nor tell you what happened to their Detective either.

But, I find some interesting cases in my line of work.

Myth-wise, you're looking at a poltergeist. The word is German in origin and literally means "noisy ghost."

What sets them apart from normal ghosts is that they tend to be much more violent. Lore says they are not something you want to encounter. They will cause any kind of trouble they can. Loud noises, throwing objects around, making a mess, levitating people or knickknacks. Trouble. They tend to haunt people more than they do places.

Such cases almost exclusively turn out to be natural. Frank Podmore, a Victorian psychical researcher, coined the "Naughty Little Girl" theory, as the "poltergeist" almost exclusively turned out to be little girls throwing things. That doesn't apply to this case, however.

If Lambert's theory that underground water caused stress on buildings which then cased "poltergeist" activity weren't already so doubtful, it wouldn't apply here. Neither do Persinger's seismic theory nor Turner's ball lightning theory (ball lightning can't be responsible for half of what it's blamed for). Let's leave suspected psychokinesis to the side.

Where does that leave us?

I couldn't say. I'd recommend looking into the police failure in the Thornton Road poltergeist, and planning a more thorough approach.

The odd thing about this case is how did Miss Watkins get away? After her attack, there were two victims in the same place in the same room in a similar manner. Both died. Did the UnSub refine their approach? It's intriguing that both victims were males, whereas a female escaped. That would be my first step in putting together a profile.

I'll attach a few articles about poltergeists for your to forward to the detectives along with my assessment.

Locked Room cases. I've wondered if they actually happened. But there has to be some sort of trick, some something that makes it make sense.

But like I said, without being there in person, I can't tell you much more. I'm a little jealous though, an actual locked room case and I have to sit it out.

Best of luck,
Rosella

Doppelgangers
(And Other Artistic Piffle)

James Bojaciuk

Apologies to Lonnie Nadler and Abby Howard

> "'I didn't know what to do, so I came straight
> to you.' That was always the way. Folk who
> were in grief came to my wife like birds to a
> light-house."
> —"The Man with the Twisted Lip," John H.
> Watson, M.D

I may rarely step inside my husband's
examining room, but I have learned to diagnose
patients from their sounds alone. Mrs. Hallard's
cough, clearly an ordinary cold which didn't
demand any medical attention. Stern words for
her. She would have aided her recovery best by
staying in bed. Mr. Habbleton's hobble—oh
dear, something gone wrong with his carriage
again, and he walked for miles. That has led to a
greater wrong in his muscles. A mild dose of
pain-reliever for him. A much stronger dose of
conversation and kindness. I pretend not to
notice when our cheque book is lighter by the
sum of an axel.

John's primary prescription, you see, is
words. I believe it must be so for all successful
doctors.

Perhaps it is also so for all successful...I do
not know what word to use for myself.

John compares me to a light-house.

I have told him I am the world's only consulting doctor's wife. We laughed.

So it was late one dreary October night, when I heard a desperate, lonely footstep up the cobblestreet, and a knock on my door, I had some impression of the matter.

Had this been Baker Street, and I had been Mr. Holmes, I could have told you any number of things—that she was an artist's wife (by a smudge of paint on her knees?), that she had been to Brighton (by the sand caught on her shoe?), and had at one time played rugby (I cannot fathom how). But *I* recognized the off-center, too-loud crack of a boot whose heel had been fixed by the owner herself, because she insisted cobblers were a conspiracy intent on parting her from her money. And *I* recognized a knock which did not recognize wood could splinter or dent.

I rose and opened the door. "Christina? Christina Thorpe, at so late an hour?"

She nodded, trying to hold back tears, then clung to me, moaning into my shoulder.

When she finally spoke, all she could say was, "It is Harold," before pressing her face into my shoulder again.

A Temperance Society matron once insisted that John must be a very poor doctor, because it seemed the only medicine he ever administered was brandy, and in "copious" amounts.

But I'm not aware of a better cure for one suffering from nerves, or a better first step to administrating kindness.

155

When Mrs. Thorpe had calmed herself, and her cling had eased into an iron grip on my hand, I heard her story. In John's fashion, I have taken the liberty of presenting what she said in a single, uninterrupted narrative. My questions, urges to continue, and fresh glasses of brandy (then, later, tea) are, I'm sure, of little interest.

"You know Harold. It is his fashion to paint with me beside him. Blank canvas is a hole in his psyche…he painted the canvas black, glancing at me, worried then furtive, before every brushstroke. He paints with such long strokes. But these were so short. He held himself back.

"A week ago he barred his studio to me. You are aware the degree to which that is alien…and he insisted it would damage my constitution! He is not such a man…and the things he has painted by my side. You have seen more than all but the European galleries, and can likely imagine the rest.

"He insisted that if I must see it, then I could only see it at the unveiling to our friends. The telegrams were sent and we had a tense dinner indeed, for I had given them some idea of the strain upon him. It was our usual party. Laurent, Zahn, Jackson, and Greystoke.

"All my husband could be compelled to say was, 'I hope you will continue to be my friends.'

"When we entered the studio, the painting hung in his preferred display space. About twelve feet above us. He stood in his workshop alcove, the only place he would ever stand to view his art. He pulled the lever to reveal it.

"He watched us all the while, sweating, the unhappiest man I have seen.

"But he needn't have worried.

"Jackson held her hand to her mouth, eyes wide. Zahn simply said nothing, blinking and trying to understand it by matching the brushstrokes with jerks of her wrist—this way then that, in sympathy. Greystoke could look nowhere else. Laurent looked like a man whose investment had paid off. It had. He has bought our paintings when we could not feed ourselves. He now held what some could call 'early works,' already more valuable by dint of this painting.

"What was it?

"All of this stress over a self-portrait!

"The most wondrous self-portrait. Loose, watercolor strokes which suggested Harold's form rather than directly state it. Stray strokes were retained as well, and a wonderful series of vertical grooves cut into the layers of paint. The texture became part of the art.

"'Astonishing,' said Greystoke.

"Harold flinched.

"'The technique…wholly inventive,' said Zahn.

"Harold leaned against the wall.

"Laurent, however, found his fullness first. 'A self-portrait beyond anything the art world can conceive of. A self-portrait beyond anything the critic or the public can conceive of. Perhaps in kind to the leap from medieval to renaissance art. The artist has wrought a miracle. The artist has made art which itself will be an artist, inspiring those who follow it. Masterpiece is too light a word.'

"Laurent is a hard man with praise. I have heard him dismiss Winslow Homer as 'paintbox dabbing' and poor Basil cried after one of his reviews. I blushed on Harold's part.

"But he was flushed altogether differently. He insisted, loudly, that 'It was not, and could not be, a self-portrait.'

"Greystoke said, 'If it was not, then he painted it with another's hand.' He smiled at his joke.

"'It is not my likeness! I have painted my Flea!'

"Zahn said, 'It is impolite to fish for compliments in this way.'

"My husband is a temperate man, sensible under all condition. But he turned his back on his painting and abandoned his alcove, marching on us in a fury. Laurent and Zahn unnecessarily blocked his way to the painting, fearing he would destroy it there.

"But with shouting, in words *I* would regret even if *he* would not, he turned them out of the house. Then he turned on me. Exhausted, but not angry, he demanded, 'Tell me truly, what did you see?'

"'A self-portrait. The finest I have ever seen.'

"He collapsed by the door.

"He then set his head in his hands and began to weep."

Here I did refill her brandy, all at once, and she looked up at me with sleepless, blood-shot eyes. "The last few days have gotten worse. The matter had seemed concluded. The room stayed locked. He refused to speak about it, though he slept poorly and ate little. He sat in the room outside his workshop, facing the door, in weary thought. I had begun to calm him to come away from there, but…

"Then they came.

"The critics. The reporters. The commentators, the gallery-men, the representatives of interested families too good to step onto our property without invites. They converged upon our home, congregating in our yard. Requests to see 'the masterpiece' were little more than demands. Harold crouched in our vestibule, pulling his hair.

"I dismissed them. It took longer than it should have. An afternoon into evening.

"I came back in to find my husband missing. He was not in sight. He did not respond to my calls. When I found him he was in the larder, still crouched, staring everywhere at once.

"'Do you hear it? Do you?'

"I pulled his hands away from beating his head and brought him to bed.

"I do not believe I had seen Harold cry until then. I do not know what I even ask of you, Mary, but…could you come home with me? Someone I can trust. John, too, when he is home. Harold needs a doctor. But I—he is sitting before the painting, drunk, with a box of matches in one hand and a cheque in the other. He will not tell me who has given it to him. He cries that the painting shifts before his eyes, melting from one face to another…please."

I hushed her, and summoned a carriage. She only stared into the hearth until I collected her.

The door was not locked. While that may have concerned an urban doctor's wife, it posed no concern to an artist's wife from the finer districts.

I followed her, first into the hall then into the sitting room, then into the study as her step faltered.

"I told him to wait. I told him never to worry me like this again."

I heard her sucked-in breath over her rush up the stairs.

She ran down the hall, glancing into every room, more harried every moment. Electric lighting makes such a process much faster than it would otherwise be. She reached for the switch, hardly reacting if she was shocked, glanced around the suddenly lit room, and hurried on. The lights were left on in a long row behind us, blazing our trail like breadcrumbs.

We finally found three men in the office. Harold sat, staring at a piece of paper. One hand held a pen, and the other was curled up in his hair, pulling. Laurent sat across the table, chair pulled out very far indeed, to suit his corpulence. The third man was well-known to me.

This third man, Sherlock Holmes himself, was speaking. "I am told 'Come at all speed! It means a man's life!' and find myself witness to an art deal! An art deal over some deathly painting—a supposed deathly painting which I am not allowed to inspect. This is madness. I am a loose end."

Laurent stirred himself up in the chair, fixing Mr. Holmes with the critical stare that bespoke doom for a disagreeing artist. "I believe that selling the painting and removing it from this house will save his life. Viewing the painting may…not have the best effect on Mr. Thorpe."

Holmes acted as though he had not noticed the look. "Then why should I be present? Is this the price of being known thanks to silly romances—to be summoned to take part in nonsensical little stories which neither concern myself nor present any interest?" He picked up his hat and cane. "Surely I would be better occupied in any opium den. I may at least *witness* a crime there."

He looked up at our entry. A genuine smile. "I see, failing to find Watson, they did not want to leave without someone bearing his name. If you would…I'm sure we could find something more amenable. Dinner at Simpson's?"

Christina rushed past Holmes, nudging him aside as she came to Harold's side. "What is this?"

Laurent leaned toward her. "Peace of mind. He has sold the painting. Now it will not worry him." He stood, tugging at his vest. "We seem to be done here. I may take it on my way out…"

Christina squinted, beginning to raise an objection, then looked down at her husband. He still tugged at his hair. "Of course. This way."

My presence seemed to have given Holmes a moment more patience—or, failing that, curiosity—and he went with the general party. His hat and gloves stayed on, and his cane in his hand.

When we reached the workshop, Mrs Thorpe once again reached for the light switch. There was a flash, then blackness.

Harold howled.

"It is only the electricity, dear." She said, brushing my arm as she tried to reach out for him.

"Yet they insist," Mr. Holmes grunted, "That electric lighting will replace gas. Too much power consumed, and it burns out. Too much strain on the system, darkness. Gas resists enemies and accident."

"It was not the breaker, I'm sure, because—" Laurent began, but…

A harsh *shhh* from Mr. Holmes. It was hardly necessary. We would have heard it even if we conversed.

Thra-thrum.

There are other sounds a doctor's wife recognizes.

Thra-thrum.

Chief among them, a heartbeat.

Thra-thrum.

It beat through the house. It reverberated the way it does through any one of our chest cavities. Being inside such a cavity, it was devastating.

Thra-thrum.

Mr. Holmes moved first. Looking above, he saw the painting was gone. The change over him was as intense as it was sudden. No longer was his evening wasted. Perhaps it was not difficult to trace it to its source. Even quieter sounds might be chased to their origin. But it was bewildering, and frightful, as Mr. Thorpe quailed, staring everywhere as if beset by a frightful enemy. Mr. Holmes sprang out of the room and we did well to follow.

My chief impression was not of the heartbeat itself, but of a scratching below the heartbeat. A maniac scratching his skin.

My whole world became that noise.

Thra-thrum.

Scitch.

I have no recollection of the walk. The noise, cloying, made me look about as Mr Thorpe.

Thra-Thrum

Scitch.

And the scratching, the omnipresent scratching, became the chief noise.

Thra-scitch-thrum.

Thra-scitch-thrum.

Thra-scritch-thscritch

Thrascritchscritch

It seemed to be breaking down, falling to pieces.

We stopped at the door to the workroom and Mr. Holmes shoved it open.

Thrscriiiiitch.

Holmes quickly took the room in, springing across.

Scriiiiiiiiiiiiiiiiitch.

An ear-destroying grind and all was silent.

We were silent for two reasons.

First, the silence that always falls upon a group when an uncanny sounds ends.

Second, the room was soaked in blood.

It was no small quantity. The blood of two strong men, perhaps three, soaked the room as though thrown across in a bucket of whitewash. It covered the floor and one wall. Ruined papers scattered the desk; one, hanging halfway off, dribbled blood onto the floor.

The portrait rest on the ruined wall. It remained untouched. But misshapen handprints had grabbed the frame. Their stains clung. The blood exploded down across the wall.

Misshapen footprints ground out of the blood, leaving a trail across to the aerie.

The painting hung, awkward, at an angle.

"Did you not say that this was a self-portrait?" It was an odd detail to fixate upon. But amid the horror, I believe I chose the most common and ordinary detail to preserve my sanity.

With that, the second, greater horror arose. Harold hurled himself to his knees. "It's gone. It's gone. It's gone."

Mr. Holmes bent down into the blood, with no concern for the state of his trousers. He prodded at it, treating his finger as a brush. Meanwhile, Laurent examined the ruined papers and work on the table. He approached Christina, taking her arm. He seemed to be convincing her to leave.

"I would be at peace if John were here," I told Mr. Holmes. "With his service revolver."

He looked up at last. "I would only be at peace if he brought his service paint thinner." He laughed, and held out his hand. "It is only paint. Someone has done a poor job of it." He stood, pants and coat tails in a truly horrendous state, and clapped his hands to shake the paint away. "I should have expected cow's blood, or pig's blood—any unsellable leftover of the butcher's trade, which most could be compelled to part with for a ha'penny. Instead, paint. Expensive paint, as well." He clicked his tongue, raising his voice to alert the others. "There is nothing to show concern over. It is *paint*."

Harold threw himself at the table, raking papers into the muck. "Of course it is paint, man! My doppelganger is paint! I made him! He has crawled out after remaking the painting into me." He began to beat his head again. "He has come out I must go in he has come out I must go in he has come out I must go in"—Christina held his hands again, firmly.

Mr. Holmes stared down at him, and murmured, "What a blessing the art in *my* blood manifested in reason." Then, louder, "Why would a spirit be well-heeled?"

"Excuse me?" Laurent said.

Mr. Holmes waved over a footprint. "Our spirit has a very fine cobbler looking after his feet, you see. It's hardly any sort of..." he paused, investing the word with disgust. "A doppelganger."

Harold sank to his knees, then onto his face. "It is my feet. It is becoming me. For God's sake."

"No," Holmes said. "Your feet are much smaller."

Christina pulled him out of the paint, drying his face with her handkerchief. "It is deformed. It is trying to become me."

"Surely that would not extend to his…" Holmes looked at the man with some kindness at last. "No, surely, if your flea were deformed, he would not simply wear larger shoes."

"You heard his heartbeat!"

"I heard an approximation of a heartbeat, yes."

It was an ill-chosen word. One so ill-chosen I cringed when he said it. "Approximation" was all that Harold's fancy needed to feed on, and from as great an authority as Sherlock Holmes, no less.

"Yes…" He stirred. "It is an approximation of my own heartbeat."

The mistake dawned on Mr. Holmes, but too late. It was all we could do was to settle him into his bed. Then, showing how much he had become invested in these strange events, he requested to see the painting. And so, we returned to the display room.

Perhaps, two hundred years ago or more, when London sprawled to a more seemly distance past its Roman barriers, this room had been a church. A place for the traveling vicar to give his sermon, when this was still a house in the country.

Dark wood—nearly black—paneling ran from the floor to the vaulted arch above.

Stepping out on its floor sounded different. The wood was hard. It did not give. And in that lack of give, it echoed.

Pews, altar, and vestments of the church were all quite cleared away. All that marked this as a church, beyond the conspicuously high ceiling, were the two alcoves. Both were separated off from the rest of the room by a low, knee high, railing. The main floor was empty. The leftmost alcove was empty. The rightmost was an artist's aerie. Paints, canvases, and all the stock of the artist's trade lay littered about. They had the touch of the theatrical. This was not an artist surprised in his work; this is an artist who wanted to seem surprised in his work. A wife knows. It was not so different from when John is reading sea stories but leaves *The Lancet* open. The primary difference between our home and this, aside from size and grandeur, was the thick layer of paint.

Mr. Holmes had already strode across the room, every step audibly sticky, and looked up. The painting hung at an unusual angle, presenting itself from the left-edge. This had been mounted in what had once been the sanctuary, where the crucifix would have stood. It still displayed what had been the self-portrait, but now was only an empty room.

An empty, lit room with a returned painting. Mr. Holmes stopped. He returned to the doorway and turned off the light. The painting seemed to disappear.

"We enter deep waters. He always displays his work so high, Mrs. Thorpe? I will answer everything when I have answers."

After a moment, she regained hold of herself. "Yes. He…thought it best to examine his work for imperfections at a museum's vantage point." Christina had come to guide Holmes on his second inspection. It should have been Laurent, by any reasonable means, but Harold had expelled her from the room, preferring to speak to Laurent.

"Museums are not accustomed to mounting art so high." Mr. Holmes stared up.

"They are for masterpieces, Mr. Holmes."

"Surely, even your husband would have noticed if men replaced his painting. This could not be easily moved. I doubt you were absent for sufficient time for this to be accomplished. How could they replace it with another painting?"

I stared at the mount, then at the floor, then at Harold's accustomed spot. An idea began to form itself. But the conversation had carried on, while I looked at that spot.

"Do you know what the beating heart was? Surely it's not…"

Then I took a few steps into the paint, hiking my skirts.

He looked at her, deciding what to say. "It was a record. A cheap, wax record. Wax is a preferable material, of course, because as the record plays—the wax simply breaks down. Sound ultimately ceases altogether. It's far easier than trying to rig a timed stop. Hence the scratching that was introduced into the sound. A basic amplifier is all one would need. All one must do is set it spinning, even better if it's somehow triggered remotely, by, say—"

"Mr. Holmes, come here." I directed him to my side. "The painting appears different from here." It was very little. The color seemed off, as though mixed with another pallet. But only at the most precise angle.

He tilted his head, first this way then that. He grinned, dashing to the far side of the room.

"It is not all in Mr. Thorpe's mind, then. Rest assured, your husband is not mad. Only preyed upon. Let us see what is really at work, shall we?"

He approached the sanctuary, climbing on what once had been the altar to tilt the painting.

"If you would press yourself against the wall, and look at the painting from your new vantage point…"

I have learned to trust Mr. Holmes' impressions. I did so, and gasped. As the painting was tilted, I could now see the self-portrait which everyone had so applauded. "I see the self-portrait, with Harold's image."

He grunted, from the altar, and leaned over. Tilting it further so that he could see. He blocked the painting entirely. Then, he turned it further. Perhaps it was an insight, or perhaps it was simply thoroughness. The noise Mr. Holmes made was a disgust that I have not heard him make over dead bodies. He shook his head, and finally looked away.

"Mrs. Watson, steel yourself and lean against the wall once more. Mind, steel yourself."

I took the requested step. I do not say what I say out of pride, but simply so that you may understand my reaction. John and I have done what we can for the "matchstick girls" afflicted with phossy jaw. Not merely monetarily, but as one of the few clinics still prepared to do what we can, in any way. Thus I am well-acquainted with distortions of the body. Perhaps it was the subject, or perhaps it was horror visited *by choice*, and on dead canvas instead of a God-breathed soul who can be reached with kindness and care.

But my stomach turned to queasy stone and I struggled to stay facing it.

It presented a man, in ordinary street dress. His skull was split bloodily open, fractured pieces falling inside. Two hands reached up from the inside, desiccated, pulling themselves over the sharp edges of his skull. These hands bled. Something suggestive of the man's own face glared up from the inside, and I wondered if I did recognize a hint of self-portraiture. Bodies lay across the street behind him, men and women, their skulls in similar states.

"It is…supposed to be Athena and Zeus?"

"Even if guessing were not destructive to the faculties…I could not."

"He was correct. It is his flea."

Mr. Holmes tilted it back, putting it up on the wall. Christina had no reaction. Not at first. It took a moment for her to find her voice. "How was such a thing…accomplished?"

Holmes moved back down to the floor, sliding along the altar. He was now covered in paint. "Easily enough. You yourself told us your husband has been experimenting with new mediums. Painting on plaster mounted on canvas. Someone has carved grooves in the plaster. I suspect your husband, trying to reach his effect. I do not know if the grooves were always angled, or if someone has come after and angled them. But the base of these grooves have been painted. Painstaking work, but simple enough to accomplish. What you see depends entirely on the angle from which you view the painting. If you see it from the right, you see your husband's intended work. If you see it straight on, directly down into the grooves, you see the marvelous self-portrait, with which everyone was so fascinated. If you see it from the left, as we lately have, the same self-portrait, minus the self. Any knowledge of your husband's viewing habits would aid the hoax."

"But…why?"

"The trick could only last so long before someone discovered it. It only takes a cursory examination. The key would be to delay such an examination. Such as by convincing the artist he has gone mad, through hoaxes both auditory and physical. There is only one person here who has any reason to do such a thing."

She nodded, about to say his name.

But there was another scream, distant and weak, from the stairway.

We ran, fearing the worst.

In the darkness, we found Harold on the stair. He had collapsed, head against the bannister. There was paint slathered about.

"I am blessed to see you one final time. I will fade away, my dear. Do not be concerned. I do not think he is a monster."

"Who?" Mr. Holmes asked.

"My double. He has emerged. I will live on as art, and art shall live on as me. I will live inside the painting. My flea will be me. It is…perhaps the best arrangement. We have spoken on the stair."

"Could you see him?"

"What would be the point? I screamed, but there is no reason to feel fear. I have known him for a long time. We spoke as friends."

Laurent coughed. There was no telling where he had emerged from. "It has always been one of Harold's preferred themes. The most recent painting I bought, of his, is a man meeting his double in the rain. The double was his shadow-self, twisted and depressed."

Christina stared at him. "You commissioned that subject."

Laurent glared at her, rather theatrically.

But it was Harold who spoke, his voice weak. "I would not have painted it, if it did not interest me. And now we know why it interested me. It has been in me, seeking to emerge, for a long time. I have accepted my duty. The world requires art. I hope he is good to you, when he fully emerges…"

That was the knife through her heart. She sank down on his shoulders, sobbing. Laurent departed, hardly looking their way. We stayed longer.When it became clear that this scene would not alter, and Christina looked up at us to leave, Mr. Holmes touched my shoulder and urged me out into the hall.

"What will we do now?"

"We shall have a talk with Mr. Laurent. We shall have a talk with the author of this destruction."

Yet another unlocked door, and one which Holmes entered without even a consideration of a knock. We entered a study which branched off the hall, lit solely by a burning hearth. It was comfortable. Laurent sat on his couch, staring at his "charity" painting with some relish.

"Did you expect I would not solve it? It was an obvious gambit. I have had the blackest of criminals hire me to cast suspicion off. But I have never seen them so nakedly go about their work once I had arrived."

"I had no intention of deceiving you."

It was one of the few times I have seen Holmes surprised. Truly surprised.

Laurent waved his cigar, and laughed. "I needed the money. Surely, you've put together my motive?"

"To drive up the value of the paintings you've bought."

"Of course. Living artists are worth nothing. Van Gogh kept chickens dry. Dead artists are worth more, of course, but they require an interesting life. Something Harold lacked. Murder makes an artist interesting, but improper. Anything venial will sell papers—not art. But a mad artist, driven mad by the power of his own work...Goya was nothing without his psychoses. Toulouse-Lautrec's been driven to a drunken haze by virtue of his shortness—that will pay dividends. *Our* madman will pay greater dividends. A small stature is humorous. Believing you traded places with your art, well…"

Laurent stood. "I am not sure if there is even something in the statues against what I've done. I haven't so much as broken-in, let alone done anything else our Metropolitan Police should judge a crime. I made a mess with some paint. I had a fairly loud machine on the premises. I have committed no worse crime. You even denied me sale of the three-fold painting, which is a pity, but shouldn't be that significant a dent when I sell the painting that *began* his obsession."

"The assault in the stairwell, surely," I said.

"No. I was still in his room; he said he was going to fetch his wife. I believe he had a genuine psychotic break. Or his doppelganger *did* emerge from the painting and strangle him." When he saw we did not share his merriment, he shrugged. "But whether I am *briefly* in the stocks or not—oh, I suspect the involvement of the great Sherlock Holmes will drive the price another twenty percent beyond the price I have named. Ten thousand on a single painting. Here, I believe, an American would whistle."

He paused, meeting Holmes' stony glare. "Thirty percent gain, then? Surely you don't think you're worth more."

"That is why you summoned me."

"Of course. The Empire fairly sparks with your name. I had hoped for Doctor Watson. But I think this shall be an even more profitable story. The case his wife solved in his stead. I expected an additional, oh, five percent for the doctor's presence. You may be worth an additional ten percent." He grinned at me. "I may clear twenty thousand pound profit on your account, my dear."

Holmes motioned toward the painting. "May I?"

Laurent nodded, great approval, admired at the painting. He seemed to be memorizing it.

"It is a pity."

"Hardly. I do not bear a grudge. I may let you have it at a discount. I bought it for thirty pounds. You are a man of means. Five thousand, as a memento of the man who used you?"

Though I have known Mr. Holmes for years, this was the first time I saw what my husband means when he describes him as "quick." John tarries over his manuscripts. He is a careful chronicler. But if there is any point where John's writing is insufficient, it rests on that word.

The painting was already in his hands. Neither Laurent nor I could have said "he picked it up."

Mr. Holmes hurled it into the fire. Confused by something other than lumber, the flames cracked the oil and devoured the canvas. By the time Laurent was on his feet, the painting was reduced to its frame and corners of canvas.

Laurent sprung past him, thrusting his hands into the fire, scooping out the remains, handful after handful. He collapsed on his knees, and thrust a pile of cinders to the carpet. I could hear it sizzle. His hands…A doctor's wife is more than able to recognize damage. I wondered if he could continue his own career.

Mr. Holmes stared down at him with repulsion. He removed a card from his breast pocket, and left it upon the mantel.

"I suspect there will be a lawsuit. You may contact my solicitor at that address. Well, I am prepared to pay whatever it was worth. Thirty pounds, yes? It was only a charity commission, after all." His laughter was bitter. "Come, Mrs. Watson."

To: Special Agent Audrey Wednesday
From: Dr. Rosella Tassoni
Subject: So Called Historical Evidence
Regarding Sherlock Holmes

Let's start this letter off by stating that I believe Sherlock Holmes is real as much as I believe in that calorie-free chocolate. The so-called evidence of his existence is circumstantial at best (the estate in Sussex, the apartment on Baker Street [which is a reconstruction and even people who believe in Holmes question the validity of]), and accounts by people whose existence cannot be verified. The locations do not exist, the people cannot be found in the historical record, and the fate of nations were seemingly decided by events which we have no other source of. Never mind that sometimes the stories appeared under Watson's name, or the city of London mourned Holmes in such black-clad droves that even the mightiest city on earth stood still for an entire day. We have our own cultural delusions.

I acknowledge that while your forensics team might have confirmed that this manuscript was written in the early 1890s, has anyone considered that the author of this may have simply wrote it to cash-in after Doyle had killed his character?

Not much is known these days about Harold Thorpe. From what I've heard about him, people claimed her went mad. This piece presents an interesting theory as to why. I'm certain the Smithsonian will get quite a few people to visit thanks to this connection with the so-called Great Detective, but I sincerely doubt they have anything to worry about from any hauntings. Even if this story had a word of truth to it.

The word Doppelganger has its origins within 100 years of this story's writing. It's German, literally meaning "double-goer." The dictionary defines it as "an apparition or double of a living person."

It was often related to the idea of evils twins, alter egos, or spirits who took the form of their victims.

It's popular theory these days that everyone has a doppelganger of sorts. That is to say, that everyone has a twin that eerily resembles them. I've heard reports of people claiming I look like an actress in Italy, for example. To the validity of that statement, I'm not entirely sure if I believe it. Obviously, another cultural delusion.

While the word Doppelganger is only a couple hundred years old, the idea of a twin, double, alter ego, or evil spirit mimicking the form of its victims is not a new concept. You can trace that throughout human history in religion, folklore, and cultural traditions.

It was particularly popular in the Victorian era. Yes, this is where I'm expected to mention Stevenson's Jekyll and Hyde, but that was an allegory. There are hundreds—if not thousands—of cases of supposed doppelgangers in Victorian Great Britain. Some run exactly as expected, with people meeting or hearing about their double. More outré cases involve such things as psychic tigers. Harold Thorpe may have gotten off lightly.

Ultimately, this is simply a short story from the period and certainly not proof of Sherlock Holmes.

Oddly enough, this isn't a myth I've had personal experience in. I do know the lore but actually had to prepare a packet instead of sending you one of my traditional standbys for this. Feel free to pass it on to the Baynes daughter. You mentioned she had some fascination in this case and Heaven forbid I not help a young mind in its quest for learning.

Tuttle & Gretel

D.J. Tyrer

The girl looked as if she had drowned: her clothes and hair were sodden and her skin pale. Normally, Jackson wouldn't have even given picking up a hitchhiker a second thought—there were so many stories about picking up someone who seemed decent and God-fearing only for them to gut you half an hour later—but the girl...she looked so forlorn and frail out there, beyond the wipers, that he could neither imagine her doing him harm nor, in good conscience, him leaving her standing in the rain.

Besides, he had both a genuine bowie knife and a Colt Python hidden down the side of his seat.

He made his decision, flicked his blinker on, slowed and pulled up beside her. He leaned across the cab and opened the door for her.

She looked up at him with pale-blue eyes that, with the pale skin and lightness of her blonde hair, made it seem as if the rain had washed away her colouring. That she was wearing faded jeans and denim jacket only added to the impression.

"You want a ride?"

She didn't answer, just stared up at him. He thought he saw a flicker of fear in her eyes. He guessed she'd probably heard some similar stories to those he had and was imagining he was some sort of serial killer. He'd read women generally preferred to take lifts with women. Probably men did, too, but did the women stop for them?

"It's okay, I don't bite." He smiled in what he hoped was neither a threatening nor leering manner. "I'll be stopping at Driberg—there's a truck halt there—so I can take you that far. After that, I'm headed for Atlanta, if you're headed down that way."

She nodded and clambered up into the cab beside him. He felt a little annoyed that, having thumbed for him to stop, she seemed wary of him, but started driving. She sat silently, playing with a St. Christopher medal she wore on a cord round her neck.

"Thanks," she said, breaking the silence. "There hasn't been any traffic for a while."

"You're welcome. So, where you headed?"

"Jonesboro. I didn't want to go to Smithfield."

"Jonesboro? I'll be passing by there tomorrow. If you want, I can drop you at the turnoff."

She nodded.

"I hitchhiked when I was about your age. Of course, the world was a safer place back then. Well, as long you weren't shipped out to 'Nam: things weren't so safe out there. But, here, things were safe. Or, they seemed so: but, then, it seemed as if there was a new serial killer every week and things ended up as they are today." He gave a laugh, hoping he didn't sound too old.

"You want to dry yourself off?" Jackson asked, after another period of silence. "I've got a cloth here somewhere..."

"Thanks."

He handed it to her and she wiped her face and arms and hair; she didn't look much better.

"Thanks," she handed it back.

"You're welcome. My name's Jackson, by the way."

"I'm Gretel."

"Oh, I think I know your brother."

She looked at him startled. "Do you?"

"Hansel..."

"Oh. Right."

He decided to change the subject. "Want some music?" He tapped the radio. "We've got country, country, country and, ah, country."

That brought the ghost of a smile to her lips and she shook her head. "I prefer hip-hop."

"I don't know what that is." That brought a muted laugh.

"It's just music." She fell silent again.

"We'll be in Driberg in about half an hour," he broke the silence after a while.

She nodded. "I'm glad you stopped for me. I'm not sure I would've; they say there's an escaped lunatic with a hook for a hand roaming about looking for victims."

"Do they?" He managed to stifle the urge to laugh. He'd heard the stories of Hook-Man as a kid and thought she was a bit old to believe such stories. "Besides," he added after a moment, "you don't have a hook for a hand, so I think I'm safe."

She looked down at her hands as if she'd never considered the point. "Oh, yeah."

Maybe she was a little simple, he thought.

"Well, I'm glad you didn't leave me out there for him."

"You're welcome."

That pretty much exhausted their conversation and they drove on in silence until the Driberg sign appeared out of the darkness. He turned to tell her.

Jackson nearly lost control of the truck. Gretel had disappeared. He slammed the brakes on, then looked around the cab, there was nowhere she could be hiding. The door and window were still shut: he was certain he would've noticed if she'd jumped out. Sure, you could get a bit hypnotised by the wipers sweeping back and forth, but...

He grabbed his gun and shoved it into the top of his pants, then, picking up his flashlights, opened his door and stepped down. Jackson shone the beam of the flashlight back and forth across the road behind the truck, then crouched down and shone it under the cab and trailer.

There was no sign of her.

He walked round to the other side of the truck and shone the beam over the scrub that lay beside the highway.

Still no sign of her.

Jackson shivered as he remembered other stories he'd heard. There was absolutely no way Gretel could've got out of the cab without him noticing and, at the speed they were going, she ought to have been hurt, if she'd managed to find some way he couldn't imagine. But, there was no hint she'd smacked into the asphalt.

He turned around and got into the cab. She still wasn't there, but he did spot the St. Christopher medal she'd been wearing, laying in the middle of the passenger seat. He shivered again, put the truck back in gear, and sped off, desperate to reach the sanctuary of other people and bright town lights, and leave the darkness behind.

Hurtling into the truck stop, Jackson barely avoided ploughing into the back of another truck, one of several parked up outside Mo's Diner. He didn't even think to lock the truck up as he jumped out and splashed across the gravel to the diner.

As he burst through the doors, everyone inside span round to look at him. There were a half-dozen truckers, a couple of bikers, a waitress and a cook, and the Sheriff.

"Something wrong?" the Sheriff drawled.

"Yes, yes."

"You look like you seen a ghost, Jackson," commented one of the truckers, who he thought was called Steevil.

"I think I just did."

"What?" That was another trucker, one he didn't recognise, with a northern accent.

"What I just said: I think I saw a ghost."

"Really?" The cook was sceptical. Some of the truckers seemed to share his view, while the others and the waitress looked open to the idea. The sheriff and the bikers kept their expressions unreadable.

"Yes, really."

"What happened?" The waitress, eyes wide, poured him a mug of coffee.

"I picked up a hitchhiker. Called herself Gretel. Said she was going to...ah, Jonesboro. Then, well, she, ah..."

"What?" asked the waitress, eyes even wider.

"Don't tell me she vanished." The cook shot him a sceptical look.

Jackson nodded. "Exactly."

The cook rolled his eyes. "Man, I hear that story all the time, you know; it's a regular urban legend. But, most folk have the decency to say it happened to a friend-of-a-friend. Just a silly ghost story."

The wide-eyed waitress shook her head, "Come on, they can't *all* be made up."

"It's called fiction for a reason."

"I dunno," said Steevil, "I've heard stories..."

"Exactly, stories."

"You sure you didn't drop her off?" The Sheriff looked doubtful. "I know you guys can zone out a bit when you've been at the wheel a while. It's monotonous work, especially when you're tired. Be honest, I ain't going to write you a ticket."

"No, I swear. I was in the middle of a conversation, and I was driving on at a good pace—there was no way she jumped out. She just...disappeared."

"Maybe you dropped off and dreamed her," The cook's tone was still doubtful.

"No way. Look, she left this..." He pulled out the medallion. "She was real. I didn't dream her

185

and I'm not mad and I'm not lying. It happened. *It really happened.*"

The waitress pressed the mug of coffee into his hands and told him, "I believe you."

"Thanks." Jackson took a sip. The surface of the coffee wobbled: his hands were still shaking.

The sheriff got up and headed for the door. "What you need, son, is a good night's sleep. Make sure you're properly rested before you set out tomorrow. I'd hate to have to give you a ticket. Well, my shift's over and I'm off to bed. Night all."

Jackson sat down and ordered another coffee, along with some toast. As he sat there, the others began to drift away—the truckers to sleep in their cabs, the bikers to who-knew-where—until it was just him and the two staff.

"You stay open all night, right?"

"Sure do," The waitress offered him another coffee.

He shook his head. "Do you object if I doze here?"

"You do that, hon."

"Don't tell me you're scared to go back to your cab," laughed the cook with another roll of his eyes.

"Seriously." Jackson shrugged. "Whatever happened, it scared the hell out of me. I don't want to go out into the darkness again. If I could, I'd stay up all night, but I can't really delay tomorrow, so I ought to have some sleep."

"You snooze all you like, hon."

"Yeah, whatever," the cook shot back over his shoulder heading out back into the kitchen.

Jackson had a third coffee, then, still buzzed, kept watch for a while, half expecting to see Gretel's face at the rain-splashed window.

Jackson woke to feel someone shaking his shoulder the sun was bright and he cursed as he raised his head from the tabletop.

"Son, I need to ask you some questions."

It was the sheriff.

Jackson looked up at him, feeling dazed. "What time is it?"

"Just after ten."

He swore again. "I'm late."

"But, that doesn't matter. As I said, I have some questions to ask you."

"Questions? What questions?" Then, his head cleared a little. "Is it about Gretel? You believe me now?"

"Kinda."

"Kinda?"

"Well, son, you see, a local fellow on his way to work spotted what turned out to be the body of a young woman in the scrub, just off the road. The ME puts her time of death at shortly before you piled in here last night."

The sheriff paused a moment to take the pistol from Jackson's belt. "Don't want that going off by accident."

Jackson looked at him. "Wait, you think I killed her?"

"I'm afraid so. She'd been gutted. Nasty. Now, I take it you have a knife?"

"Sure, in my cab."

"It'll have to be tested. Now, I want you to stand, and put your hands on the table."

A moment later, Jackson was in cuffs and being led out to the waiting sheriff's car, while a deputy went for his knife.

"Why on earth would you think I killed her?"

"Well, son, she had ID on her, so were able to contact her family first thing. Her poor parents were devastated..."

"So?"

"So, I noticed a mark on her neck, as if a necklace had been torn away, so I asked and what do you think they said she would've been wearing?"

"A St. Christopher's medal," groaned Jackson.

"Exactly. A young woman with a St. Christopher's medal. Just like you were carrying on about last night."

"Don't you see? It was her ghost. It really was a ghost. I told you!"

The sheriff pushed him into the backseat and said, "Now, what I think happened is this: you killed the girl. I don't know why. Maybe our ME can answer that. Anyway, you killed her. Perhaps, you didn't mean to and that's why you snapped. Or, perhaps you were trying to concoct some bizarre alibi, I don't know. But, either way, then you came in here with your crazy story."

"I didn't do it, I swear."

"Yeah, that's what they all say..."

"I have some good news and some bad news."

Jackson looked at the man appointed to defend him; a lawyer named Tyler, but said nothing. He'd given up speaking when it became clear nobody gave a damn what he said.

"The bad news is that the DA seemed determined to nail you for the murder of this girl. The good news is he's an arrogant SOB whose only evidence is that medallion doohickey you found. Yes, it connects the two of you, but it's circumstantial. You gave her a lift, she dropped it. Nobody takes a trophy from a killing, then waves it at the sheriff."

"I didn't kill her."

"I'm sure you didn't."

Jackson slammed his fist on the table. "Don't patronise me!"

Tyler held his hands up placatingly. "Sorry. Look, they have no forensics to link you to the murder: your knife isn't even similar to the one that killed her, besides being clean, and there was no DNA, fibre or anything. The DA's inventing all kinds of wild stories—he's probably invoking aliens, by now—but, I'm convinced you didn't do it, and I'll be able to demonstrate sufficient reasonable cause to get you off."

"Look, it's exactly as I said: she was a ghost."

Tyler didn't answer, but looked at him thoughtfully.

That evening, as Jackson spent yet another night in jail, Tyler reread the transcripts of his discussions with him. The man had never wavered from the story he'd told.

"She said: 'They say there's an escaped lunatic with a hook for a hand roaming about looking for victims.'"

The girl—whether living passenger or ghostly hitchhiker—hadn't said much, according to Jackson, but he'd clearly recalled her saying that.

An escaped lunatic with a hook for a hand? It sounded like some creepy campfire story, and yet...from what Jackson had said, Gretel had been young and naive. Was it possible she'd embellished a genuine news report?

Tyler picked up the phone and began making some phone calls: anyone within a couple of hundred miles he knew who had medical, psychiatric or law enforcement connections. About midnight, he had his answer.

Taking out a map of the state, Tyler located Waywood Mental Hospital. According to a state trooper over at Metford Junction, an APB had gone out for an escaped homicidal maniac. No mention of a hook, but that was just the thing a terrified kid might imagine, or might mistake a knife for, or...had she really been a ghost?

He shook his head. He was exhausted. He wouldn't normally pay heed to ghost stories. Still, it didn't really matter if she was a ghost when the truck driver picked her up. No jury was going to base its decision on that. Even if she'd been killed before Jackson said he'd picked her up, it didn't matter—all he needed to do was prove that the escapee killed her and the jury could assume Jackson got his timings wrong, gave a lift to a dead girl, or travelled through time, for all he cared.

Of course, he could get Jackson off on reasonable doubt, but he wanted to be certain, needed to show he definitely didn't do it. Besides, the girl deserved it.

Spectral testimony had been admitted at the Salem Witch Trials, but it wasn't something people were keen to listen to nowadays. Unless it came from psychics with syndicated TV shows. Had he been able to, Tyler would've been glad to hand what he knew to the sheriff or the state troopers and let them take over the hunt.

With a sigh, he put on another cup of coffee and prepared to look over his notes again. He had a feeling it was going to be a long night.

By the time he was down to the dregs in the pot, he was beginning to think he was wasting his time. But, there was one thing that was niggling at him. He slipped a piece of nicotine gum into his mouth, massaged his temples and decided to make this the last pass before he locked up his office and headed home.

Checking back through the transcripts, Tyler spotted another oddly-specific piece of information Jackson had recounted; namely that the girl had very specifically said she didn't want to go to Smithfield. If Jonesboro was her destination, who'd wanted her to go there? It was a long shot, but...

He packed up. He needed to sleep, refresh himself. Then, he could follow up on his hunch.

Tyler set out early.

A Google search had found only one place called Smithfield in the state, a plantation that appeared to be uninhabited. If there was any truth to what Jackson had said, this had to be the place. It was going to be a long drive.

Tyler yawned and plucked his coffee from the car's cup holder. He didn't feel refreshed. He took a sip. It had been drizzling when he set out and the wipers had a soporific effect. Finally he flicked them off as the sun warily emerged from behind the clouds.

At his satnav's command, he turned off the highway and was jolted to full wakefulness by the bumpy road.

The branches of overhanging trees slapped at the car. The road was little more than a line of gravel between the fields, muddy in parts where the stones had been scuffed away. The occasional wooden shack he passed appeared derelict, their plots overgrown, and the telegraph poles that ran alongside the road were denuded of their wires. He didn't see another car or anyone working the land. The whole county gave the impression of being abandoned.

His cell phone rang. It was his assistant, Christie.

"Hey, what have you got?" He'd sent her to the records office in the state capital.

"You were right. Tuttle"—that was the escapee—"has a connection with Smithfield. His great-aunt was the last owner."

"Hot dog! Right, call the state troopers and let them know he might be hiding out there."

The satnav sent him down a side road that was little more than a dirt track, a muddy slough after the rains that had been falling intermittently for days. After half a mile, it ended at a swollen stream. What should have been a picturesque covered bridge had collapsed in upon itself and become cloaked in vines.

Tyler swore and slapped his dashboard. There was no way he was getting across. He was going to have to find another way around.

He drove back down the track and onto the gravelled road before resetting his satnav. It took him a little further along the highway, then down some country back roads almost as poorly maintained as the one that had led him to a dead end.

He was growing near Smithfield. His satnav announced a left turn and he found himself bumping his way along an overgrown dirt track.

Then, he saw the plantation house. It was on a rise above the low-lying country about it. Once tall and white, the building was in a state of collapse and what paint was left had tarnished to a dirty grey. Trees clustered in close about it, the garden and fields that surrounded it having long ago been returned to nature.

He pulled up some distance away. His car just wasn't going to make it any further up the steep and heavily-rutted track and, ideally, he needed the state troopers to locate and arrest the escapee, Tuttle. Tyler didn't really want to take the risk of a confrontation if he didn't have to. Best to wait where he was.

Still, he took a gun from his glove compartment, just in case, a .38 snubnose revolver.

He drummed his fingers on the dashboard, nerves and impatience mixing. He popped a piece of nicotine gum into his mouth, the chewing helping to calm his nerves.

Then, he noticed movement on the edge of his vision. It was past the house, down a vague track, where he guessed the outbuildings were located. Tuttle? It had been a figure, he was certain of that. But, it hadn't seemed large and his description said he was a big man. Still, it had to be him; who else could it be? But, had Tuttle noticed him? Did he know he was here? He might have heard the engine. Tyler glanced at his watch and wondered how long the state troopers would take. Would they even come?

Tyler stepped out of his car and moved cautiously towards where he'd seen movement. There were tire marks on the damp ground. He followed the tire tracks down past the side of the plantation house. As he'd suspected, there were several outbuildings here. Most of them were wooden, some little better than ruinous heaps, but a few were made of brick or sheets of red-rusted iron. One had even been burst asunder by a tree growing from within it. There was an aura about the place, mournful and uninviting. He shuddered.

The tire tracks led him to a brick-built outbuilding that was in better shape than most of its neighbours. A pick-up truck was parked nearby. Tyler returned his gaze to the ground and spotted boot prints. The prints led between the vehicle and the building. Tuttle was clearly inside.

Tyler nervously approached the building. He looked back towards where he'd left his car, but there was no sign of any backup. It was impossible to see down to the road from where he was and he couldn't hear anything save the rustle of the breeze through the leaves of the trees and the occasional birdcall. He took out his phone, but there was no signal. He was on his own.

He took a deep breath and opened the door. The interior was dark. He had the impression of barrels and crates, but could see nothing clearly. The air smelt damp. He listened, but couldn't hear anything.

He stepped inside, took a couple more steps, then stopped. He heard a slight scuffling sound. He looked about. There was movement in the shadows. It resolved itself into the shape of a man: A man with a hook in place of a hand. Tyler took an involuntary step back.

"My name is Steven Tyler and I'm an attorney. Mr. Tuttle, state troopers are on their way. Please surrender yourself into my custody until they arrive." He sincerely wished his voice carried the authority he wished to project.

Tuttle swore and ran at him. Tyler retreated back outside.

"I have a gun and will use it to defend myself," he warned. Tuttle didn't stop, didn't seem to hear.

Tyler only got the vaguest impression of Tuttle amongst the shadows as the wild-haired madman picked up speed and let out a howl of rage, like some ghastly monster.

"I'll shoot!"

The hook-handed horror reached the doorway, burst out into the daylight and Tyler fired and fired again.

Tuttle collapsed in a heap on the ground, suddenly no more than a man. The hook, Tyler realised, was not attached to him, but a meat hook he'd been holding. A terrible weapon, but hardly that of myth. Tyler kicked it away from him.

Tuttle twitched, clinging to life.

Tyler staggered back from Tuttle, dizziness suddenly hitting him. He felt a heady mixture of relief he hadn't killed the man and a twinge of guilt that he hadn't done so. He turned away, sucking in deep breaths of damp air, attempting to regain his equilibrium. He needed to get away from here.

As quickly as he could, Tyler headed back to the front of the plantation house. Then, he took out his phone again and headed down the track until he could find a signal and, then, called the state troopers. "I have your escaped lunatic. Send an ambulance."

Reluctantly, pausing to fetch a blanket from his car, Tyler returned to the maniac's side. The man's breaths came in ragged gasps. He knelt beside him. He needed to keep Tuttle alive so that his testimony could exonerate his client. There might be forensic evidence, but would it be conclusive? He pressed the blanket against his wounds, attempting to stem the flow of blood.

The last thing Tyler wanted was for his client's freedom to depend upon the testimony of another ghost.

It was only as he thought that, that he realised Tuttle had left no footprints where he'd thought he'd seen him, the movement that had led him to Tuttle. Tyler shuddered and tried not to think of it, wishing the state troopers would hurry up. The sooner he was away from Smithfield, the better.

"I can't thank you enough," said Jackson, pumping his lawyer's hand on the sidewalk outside the sheriff's office.

Tyler grinned. "I told you, I knew you were innocent."

"Not just for me, but for Gretel."

"Sorry?" He felt a chill travel along his spine. The mention of her name only brought to mind possibilities he didn't like to confront.

"Sitting in that cell, I done me some thinking; I reckon she came to me because she wanted help—justice. And, thanks to you, she got it." Jackson sighed. "Still, if I never see another ghost, I'll be one happy trucker."

Tyler chuckled, but the sound was hollow. "I don't blame you." Then, he added, "Well, you're a free man—keep on trucking."

To: Agent Audrey Wednesday
From: Dr. Rosella Tassoni
Subject: Smithfield Case

I'm fairly certain I've told you and Agent Pugsley several times that I will not report whether or not a ghost is real. That being said, here's my thoughts on this case, I hope it helps you tie the loose ends in that investigation.

It sounds like you have a case of a Vanishing Hitchhiker. This is also known as the Ghost Hitchhiker, the Phantom Hitchhiker, and the Woman in White.

Jan Harold Brunvand, author of *The Vanishing Hitchhiker: American Urban Legends and their Meanings*, described it as "the most often collected and the most discussed contemporary legend of all."

Unlike most modern ghost stories, this one is one of the more mellow ones. The Vanishing Hitchhiker usually does not have the gore of some other ghost stories.

A thing to note is that like Gretel, many versions of the lore center around grief. Either they can't let go, or they feel the need to finish the task they were doing when they died, or (as in this particular case) they cannot rest until their killer is brought to justice.

As you did ask me to explore any options that came to mind—perhaps Jackson saw something that his mind blocked out and replaced with the illusion of Gretel. There have been cases of one's mind replacing something traumatic with something less so but some of the details leak through.

Was the ghost of Gretel real?

That is not in my job description.

Either way, at least this case was able to be solved.

Hope this helps,
Rosella.

Contributors

M.H. NORRIS is an award-winning mystery maven and sci-fi sorceress. She is 18thWall Productions' Public Relations Liaison, *The Time Travel Nexus*' Television Coordinator, the co-host/producer of *The Raconteur Roundtable*, and the author of the award-winning *Badge City: Notches* (Best Novella—The Pulp Ark New Pulp Awards 2016), and *The Whole Art of Detection* (#4 Best Mystery Novel—The Preditors and Editors Readers' Poll 2016). Her short fiction has appeared in *The Lemon Herbets*, *Speakeasies and Spiritualists*, *Saucy Robot Stories*, and *Glass Coin*. Her all-new mystery series, *All the Petty Myths*, will appear later this year. You can always find her on Twitter as @MHNorris4.

MARC SORONDO lives with his wife and children in New York. He loves to read, and his interests range from fiction to comic books, physics to history, oceanography to cryptozoology, and just about everything in between. He's a perpetual student and occasional teacher. For more information, go to MarcSorondo.com.

JAMES BOJACIUK is 18thWall Production's Chief Executive Officer Duobus. His fiction and articles have appeared in *Speakeasies and Spiritualists*, the Faction Paradox anthology *Stranger Tales of the City*, *Occult Detective Quarterly*, *greydogtales*, *The Time Travel Nexus*, *Sargasso: The Journal of William Hope Hodgson Studies*, & many other publications in print and online.

He has curated the Sherlock Holmes collection*, The Science of Deduction*, and *Cryptid Clash!* (with Josh Reynolds).

He is one of the co-hosts and co-producers of *The Raconteur Roundtable*, and finds himself on a number of other podcasts.

He is also relentlessly busy, grows a fine Indiana Jones stubble, would like to own bearded dragons, and is famous for finding his story absent from this ARC.

DJ TYRER is the person behind Atlantean Publishing and has been widely published in anthologies and magazines around the world, such as *Chilling Horror Short Stories* (Flame Tree), *State of Horror: Illinois* (Charon Coin Press), Steampunk Cthulhu(Chaosium), *Tales of the Black Arts* (Hazardous Press), *Ill-considered Expeditions* (April Moon Books), and *Sorcery & Sanctity: A Homage to Arthur Machen* (Hieroglyphics Press), and in addition, has a novella available in paperback and on the Kindle, *The Yellow House* (Dunhams Manor).

DJ Tyrer's website is at http://djtyrer.blogspot.co.uk/

Acknowledgments

To my mom: who has put up with quite a bit while I've started off a career in writing. Thank you so much for everything. Thanks for ignoring all the notes about murder all over and the obsessive stacks of books I've seemed to accumulate. Love you lots.

To my dad: Thanks for the encouragement and for making sure that that one county in Kentucky is full of my books.

To Grammy: The Mary in Mary Helen, for those of you who don't know. I'm so proud to be named after such an amazing strong woman. Thank you for your encouragement all these years and for always teaching me that through hard work and perseverance you can't accomplish a lot.

To Joseph and Sam: You two are awesome brothers. Love you lots.

To Fraaaand: Yes, I couldn't resist that Jamie. Thanks for driving on some of our roadtrips so I could sit on my laptop and type away.

To James, Nikki, Ben, and the 18thWall crew: It's been quite an adventure. Can't wait to see where the road ahead leads. Thanks for helping bring this book to life.

To T.J. and Marc: Thank you guys for your patience as everything that could go wrong with this book seemed to go wrong. It's finally here!

To Pam: Thanks for putting up with an unsure author who didn't know what she wanted on her cover.

To Shoshana: There aren't words to express how thrilled I am that you drew one of my covers. Thank you so much for helping us out and if I need to apologize to Erik for you taping the pentagram to the floor to make sure you got the cover right, let me know.

Preview
Inzignanin
Josh Reynolds

Coming soon from 18thWall Productions, the final volume of Cryptid Clash!'s first series, Josh Reynold's *Inzignanin*. Lizard Man vs the Third Eye Man for the fate of the world.

One

Columbia, South Carolina,
February 1865

Henry Orr stood in the dark, surrounded by desperate men. Above him, the city where he'd been born was dying. It was not a slow death, or a kind one. It was brutish, nasty and short. But perhaps it could yet be averted.

Columbia sat upon soft ground, and had set its roots deep. Hernando de Soto had warred with the Cofitachequi here, and the bones of savages were the foundations of these catacombs. The ancient stonework dripped with moisture, and insects hummed beneath low, utilitarian arches. These were not the grandiose catacombs of Paris, or the underworld of London. Instead, they were brick corpse roads, narrow avenues stretching from the Congaree

River to somewhere beneath the college. Horse drawn carriages used them on occasion, as did soldiers, but these days they were empty of all save supplies for the war effort. Bales of cotton, and boxes full of blockade-run ammunition.

Not enough of the latter, though. Never enough. The blue bellies had three men for every one cartridge the quartermasters could supply. Soon though, such trivialities wouldn't matter none. Orr smiled, thinking of what was to come.

"If you're going to do something, Orr, you'd best get to doing. Mayor Goodwyn has already ridden out to hand the city over to the damnyankees. And Beauregard ain't coming back, not with Sherman snapping at his tail."

Orr turned. The man in gray was tall and blocky, with a face like well-chewed meat. Jeremiah Boan had seen the elephant, and had the rank to prove it. One hand rested on the Kerr's Patent Revolver holstered on his hip. Boan hadn't come down here alone. Men in butternut and gray, or blue wool scavenged from the ashes at Rivers Bridge and Aiken. All of them had the starved, haunted look of men on the edge of defeat. They sat or stood as far away as they could get, and spoke softly of anything but what was going on in the chamber. There were some things a sensible man didn't want to see.

"Goodwyn's a damn traitor," Orr said, as he began to unbutton his shirt. "Hampton should have shot him." The air was muggy and damp, and it was almost a relief to go without a shirt. He'd chosen this place because it was close to the river, and deep enough that that war wouldn't reach them for some time. Too, certain things were best done in concealment.

"Hampton should have done a lot of things," Boan said. "Maybe we all should've. But it's too late for regrets now, ain't it, Mr. Orr?"

"Call me Henry, please." Orr stripped off his shirt and tossed it aside. His bare arms and torso were marked with a mixture of henna and dog's blood in the proper fashion, as derived from the *Libre Ivonis* and the *Liber Armadel.* "We are about to undertake the ultimate adventure, sir, and we should be friends."

"You're a damn witch-man, Orr. A diabolist. We ain't going to be friends."

Orr frowned. "No, I suppose not." He gave a crooked smile. "At least we are not enemies, then. We both fight for the same cause."

"I expect not," Boan said, bluntly. "But whatever you need to tell yourself, to do this horrible thing." He cast a wary eye over Orr's preparations—the piles of books, the concentric circles of salt, blood and water, and the candles at the cardinal points, so as to honor the kings of the north, south, east and west. The blood had come from those no one would miss, and their dark bodies lay empty and still in the far corners of the chamber.

Even now, with Sherman slavering at the threshold, slaves were easy enough to come by and dispose of. Having Boan and his men around made it easier. They had been seconded to him on the orders of those in the current Confederate government disposed to heed him.

There weren't many, these days, since Grand High Magister Cottonwood had departed for unknown spheres, or perhaps San Francisco, but Orr and those like him struggled on nonetheless. They had built their shrines here, in the dark swamps and high mountains of the original colonies, and set down the foundation stones of their temples. If the Confederacy fell, those things might be lost, and all that they had achieved with them.

Orr crouched and dipped his hands in a large basin of blood, mixed with mint and waters from an unnamed lake, south of Sibiu, in Transylvania. He splashed himself five times, marking his chest and shoulders, as he'd learned in Salamanca. Boan watched him, his expression one of disgust. Orr didn't hold it against him. Small minds were quickly made, and Boan was the sort to hold tight to first impressions.

"Is all this really necessary?" Boan asked. His men stirred, as if he were articulating the unease they all felt.

"If it were not, neither of us would be here." Orr took his place at the center of the circles. He would be the aleph around which the great working would turn. His mind and soul would anchor it to this soil, to this city. He crossed his legs and folded his hands, as the black lamas had taught him, in his youthful wanderings. There were many strands to this rite, many threads pulled from different coats, but all woven together into something new.

He reached into the basin again, and retrieved that which had been steeping in it. It was an old thing, withered and as hard as stone. It was a hand—a claw, rather—and bigger than any man's, with thicker bones. Fossilized by its time in the good Carolina soil. Stiff spines of webbing thrust up between sturdy digits, tipped with hooked claws of black keratin. The claw of a more perfect predator. A thing no man could have stood against.

"What the hell is that?" Boan demanded.

"Ever read any John Mitchell Kimble?" Orr cleared his throat and recited, "The grim stranger was called Grendel, a mighty haunter of the marches, one that held the moors; fen and fastness, the dwelling of the monster race…"

Boan shook his head. "That's just a story."

"All men are but collections of their own stories." Orr ran his fingers along the sundered bones. "It took me ages to find this here lovely. Years of scrounging through accounts left by de Soto and others. The Spaniards knew of these folk, and feared them. So too did the Congaree and the Cusabo."

"It's a devilish thing," Boan said.

"So is what's happening above us." Orr looked up at Boan. "Can you smell it, Boan?"

"Smell what?" Boan looked around suspiciously.

"The smoke of fires yet to be set. The conflagration I saw in my dreams. By dusk, Columbia will be engulfed in firestorm of biblical proportions. When the dawn comes, we will be left with nothing but broken chimneys and regret. Unless I am successful."

"You still haven't explained what you—what

we—are doing down here. What kind of conjure are you working?" Boan's fingers played across his pistol. He looked as if he half-wanted to use it. Orr laughed.

"Why, I am calling for reinforcements."

"Demons," Boan said.

Orr snorted and gave the fossil a pat. "They were as one with water and land. And they ruled these parts for time out of mind. It is them to whom I shall reach out, and draw them up from the waters of black time, so that they might sweep the damnyankees from our city." He slashed the fossilized claw out, for emphasis.

"Demons," Boan said again.

"Well, they ain't angels, so I suppose," Orr said. "If you insist on attempting to define the indefinable, call them Inzignanin, for that was they called themselves when they ruled these lands. Me, I'll be content with just plain calling them up." He took a last look around, centring his thoughts. It was no easy thing to wrestle with the invisible world. And despite his bravado, he had never done this before. Nonetheless, it would work.

It must work.

He would call up the Inzignanin, and set them upon Sherman and his hellhounds. A race of dragons, set loose to burn the land clean. A great working indeed, and one which would ensure the name of Henry Orr was enshrined in the histories to come. He would be a magus to rival St. Germaine, Albertus, Prinn, even Cottonwood himself. More, he would have saved his people from the tyranny of lesser men.

"And that is all any of us can ask," Orr murmured, as he closed his eyes. He had memorized the incantations and words. Time was a funny thing, and those entities which were its masters dangerous beyond conception. Aforgomon was their master and the greatest of their number, and it was to him that Orr made obeisance.

His voice echoed back to him as it caught the angles of the chamber. The incantation was old—older even than man, at least in his current incarnation. The words were meant for cruder lips, and less genteel enunciation, but Orr made do. He wove them upon the air, phrase by phrase, and made the seventy-nine required gestures. By the end, his hands were aching, and his throat was raw, but he'd moved beyond such simple aches and pains.

It was as if his senses had expanded to fill the tunnels, for he could see every entrance, and feel the susurration of the Congaree in his very marrow. His perceptions stretched every outward, moving to quaquaversal points—up and down, east and west, until he could see the city above, as if it were phantom image, imprinted upon his eyes and mind. He could feel the creak of wagon wheels, and the dull heat of growing panic, as Sherman's forces marched on the city. Hampton was gone, galloping towards Durham.

He winced. The city bucked like a wounded animal as an explosion rocked the South Carolina Railway Depot. He saw the flicker of fading souls in the afterglow. Columbia, like all modern cities, held tight to its dead, drawing them down into its azoic foundations. Night-souled Pythagoreans had helped plan the construction of Columbia almost a century before, employing obscure metageometries to make of the city a collection of levers and fulcrums, for fell purposes of their own. But now, Orr would employ those levers to open up time itself. The city was a lock, and Orr's will, the key.

The chamber, Boan, all of it faded, like so much smoke on the wind. Orr's mind dove deep into the city's heart, seeking that which might once have ruled here. He could hear the tramp of feet, the growl of guns, the heartbeat of every man, woman and child. And something else—a pulsing, pounding rhythm, like the crashing waves of some dark sea. The oldest sea, which had once owned all the land, and given birth to all that walked and crawled. There were shapes in the deep, iridescent and round, which pulsated in time to the rhythms of the sea. Clutching the fossilized talon to him, Orr reached out with his free hand. "I see them," he said, his voice a harsh whisper. "They sleep, awaiting my call."

He heard Boan's voice, as if from a distance. "What's that smell—like a gator, crawling up out of the mud...what's that shadow?" Other voices added their own weight to his. Men were praying, whispering, crying. Small minds filled swiftly with fear.

Shapes were swimming around him, long shapes, ghostly but somehow solid for all that. The claw he held grew warm, as if blood pumped through it. Were these them, then? Had he found the Inzignanin, down in the dark? Great jaws opened, disgorging the smells of the river, and spoiled meat. He saw teeth, and felt the rough rasp of scale against stone.

"There's water," Boan said, his voice a dim bell-toll of accusation. "It's pouring from the walls, rising up from the floor. What've you done, witch-man?"

Orr ignored him. Ignored the feeling of water, pouring down his shoulders and across his chest. The shapes were coming closer now, drifting through the black, their eyes like lamps. They were like men, or dragons, or the great beasts whose bones Lewis and Clark had brought back from their time in the wilderness. And in them was a mighty hunger. He reached out to them.

"I'm ordering you to stop," Boan said. "Whatever you're calling up—send it back! Or so help me God, I'll make you do it."

The shapes circled him, rising from below, surging down from above, powerful beyond his wildest conceptions. They too were part of the city, part of the land itself. He could almost hear their voices, answering his calls. There were so many of them. An army that no man could stand against...

"God forgive me," Boan said.

Thunder boomed.

And then, only darkness.

DID YOU ENJOY WHAT YOU JUST READ?

If you enjoyed this book, *please* review it on Amazon and GoodReads!

It's the best way to support the author.

For fantastic fiction, in-depth articles by your favourite authors, open submissions, and more, please…

VISIT OUR WEBSITE
18thwall.com/

LIKE US ON FACEBOOK
facebook.com/18thwall/

FOLLOW US ON TWITTER
@18thWall

We'd love to hear from you! You help make these books possible.

www.ingramcontent.com/pod-product-compliance
Lightning Source LLC
Chambersburg PA
CBHW060641260626
47161CB00008B/2945